MONEY OR LOVE

Now Robin had finished the cheese and drained his glass of the last drop of claret.

"We will have coffee in the study," he instructed Burley as he rose from the table.

Alena followed him as he walked to the door.

As they made their way down the passage towards the study he slipped his arm through hers and exclaimed,

"I have more good news for you, Alena, and I am sure you will think I have been very clever."

"I always think so, Robin."

He smiled as he opened the door of the study and closed it behind them.

"I have had a most exciting morning," he breathed.

He strode across the room to stand in front of the mantelpiece.

"What has happened?" Alena asked quizzically.

"I went over to the American Embassy to tell the Ambassador that you and I would be delighted to dine with him tonight."

"You did not tell me he had invited us."

"I forgot. It was just a casual invitation if we were not doing anything else."

"I would rather like to see the Embassy – "

"You are not just going to see the Embassy, you are going to meet the man you will marry!"

Alena stiffened.

"You are *not* serious, Robin?"

THE BARBARA CARTLAND PINK COLLECTION

Titles in this series

MONEY OR LOVE

BARBARA CARTLAND

Barbaracartland.com Ltd

Printed and bound in Great Britain by Cle-Print Ltd.
of St Ives, Cambridgeshire.

THE BARBARA CARTLAND PINK COLLECTION

Barbara Cartland was the most prolific bestselling author in the history of the world. She was frequently in the Guinness Book of Records for writing more books in a year than any other living author. In fact her most amazing literary feat was when her publishers asked for more Barbara Cartland romances, she doubled her output from 10 books a year to over 20 books a year, when she was 77.

She went on writing continuously at this rate for 20 years and wrote her last book at the age of 97, thus completing 400 books between the ages of 77 and 97.

Her publishers finally could not keep up with this phenomenal output, so at her death she left 160 unpublished manuscripts, something again that no other author has ever achieved.

Now the exciting news is that these 160 original unpublished Barbara Cartland books are already being published and by Barbaracartland.com exclusively on the internet, as the international web is the best possible way of reaching so many Barbara Cartland readers around the world.

The 160 books are published monthly and will be numbered in sequence.

The series is called the Pink Collection as a tribute to Barbara Cartland whose favourite colour was pink and it became very much her trademark over the years.

The Barbara Cartland Pink Collection is published only on the internet. Log on to www.barbaracartland.com to find out how you can purchase the books monthly as they are published, and take out a subscription that will ensure that all subsequent editions are delivered to you by mail order to your home.

NEW

Barbaracartland.com is proud to announce the publication of ten new Audio Books for the first time as CDs. They are favourite Barbara Cartland stories read by well-known actors and actresses and each story extends to 4 or 5 CDs. The Audio Books are as follows:

The Patient Bridegroom	The Passion and the Flower
A Challenge of Hearts	Little White Doves of Love
A Train to Love	The Prince and the Pekinese
The Unbroken Dream	A King in Love
The Cruel Count	A Sign of Love

More Audio Books will be published in the future and the above titles can be purchased by logging on to the website www.barbaracartland.com or please write to the address below.

If you do not have access to a computer, you can write for information about the Barbara Cartland Pink Collection and the Barbara Cartland Audio Books to the following address:

Barbara Cartland.com Ltd., Camfield Place,
Hatfield, Hertfordshire AL9 6JE, United Kingdom.
Telephone: +44 (0)1707 642629
Fax: +44 (0)1707 663041

THE LATE DAME BARBARA CARTLAND

Barbara Cartland who sadly died in May 2000 at the age of nearly 99 was the world's most famous romantic novelist who wrote 723 books in her lifetime with worldwide sales of over 1 billion copies and her books were translated into 36 different languages.

As well as romantic novels, she wrote historical biographies, 6 autobiographies, theatrical plays, books of advice on life, love, vitamins and cookery. She also found time to be a political speaker and television and radio personality.

She wrote her first book at the age of 21 and this was called *Jigsaw*. It became an immediate bestseller and sold 100,000 copies in hardback and was translated into 6 different languages. She wrote continuously throughout her life, writing bestsellers for an astonishing 76 years. Her books have always been immensely popular in the United States, where in 1976 her current books were at numbers 1 & 2 in the B. Dalton bestsellers list, a feat never achieved before or since by any author.

Barbara Cartland became a legend in her own lifetime and will be best remembered for her wonderful romantic novels, so loved by her millions of readers throughout the world.

Her books will always be treasured for their moral message, her pure and innocent heroines, her good looking and dashing heroes and above all her belief that the power of love is more important than anything else in everyone's life.

*"All the money and riches of the world cannot buy love –
the real, true and perfect love we all strive for comes
only from God and it will always be His unique
and wonderful gift to mankind."*

Barbara Cartland

CHAPTER ONE
1891

The Solicitor finished reading the document in his hand and looked up at the couple listening to him.

"I am afraid, Sir Robin," intoned Mr. Lawson, "that you have been rather shocked by all you have just heard."

Sir Robin Dunstead, a good-looking young man of twenty-nine, replied,

"Shocked is scarcely an adequate word. Horrified and appalled is perhaps better. Actually there are no words to express what I am really feeling."

His sister Alena, sitting next him, put out her hand and laid it on his arm.

She agreed totally with what he was saying and was feeling the same herself.

But there was no point in her saying so.

"I am very sorry," continued Mr. Lawson, "and of course, unless you wish me to tell anyone what I have just told you, Sir Robin, I will keep it all strictly confidential to myself and my partners."

"That is just what I would wish," replied Sir Robin. "Equally I am wondering if you are absolutely sure there is nothing left in the house that is not entailed."

The Solicitor hesitated for a moment.

He was an elderly man with white hair and he had served Sir Robin's father for over forty years. He knew more about the family possessions than anyone else.

1

"I think," he stated solemnly after the silence had become almost unbearable, "that I must now be completely honest with you."

"I agree."

Sir Robin nodded his head.

"Speaking frankly, Sir Robin, your father has been through the entire house perhaps a dozen times looking for anything he could sell. We found some small unimportant objects, but I can assure you that there is nothing left worth more than a few pounds that is not entailed."

The eighth Baronet, Sir Edward Dunstead, had died the previous week and because he had been so ill for a long time and his son had only recently returned from India, the funeral had been a quiet one with only relatives who lived nearby expected to attend.

Robin and Alena were the only near relatives alive and as their father had been in a coma for nearly a year, it would have been untrue to pretend they were deeply upset by his death.

It was in fact a merciful relief both to the sick man and to every member of the household.

Sir Robin had not asked to meet Mr. Lawson and hear the will until today as he was quite sure that the only two people who were really interested in it would be his sister and himself.

He remembered that, when his father first became ill, he had agreed to the Solicitor's suggestion at the time.

It was that the relatives who relied entirely on Sir Edward for their income should be given the capital sum now that they would have expected on his death.

This meant his son who was serving in India would not be required to sign any more cheques that were sent out to the relatives each month.

Now when the will had been read, Mr. Lawson had made it very clear that there was nothing left.

Sir Edward, before he became ill, had spent money lavishly as if he was an immensely rich man.

And when he had no ready money, he merely sold something from the house and spent the proceeds.

Dunstead Hall in Oxfordshire was one of the most outstanding and historic buildings in the whole country.

It originally dated back to the fifteenth century and had been added to and improved, especially in the previous century.

The Adam brothers themselves had added a new façade and built on two side wings.

It seemed absurd for one man to live alone in such an enormous building, but no one in the family had been brave enough to criticise Sir Edward.

Most of them lived far away and his only son was serving in the Army in India.

His daughter, Alena, since the age of sixteen had been educated at the most select seminary for young ladies in Florence.

Because it was a long way to return home for the holidays, she had spent them with her friends in France and other countries of Europe and this had certainly enhanced her education and use of languages.

But her absence had made her completely unaware of her father's financial position.

Because of his two magnificent houses and the way he lived, she had always imagined him to be enormously rich.

Now she and her brother were told that there was nothing left but the houses and their contents – all of which were entailed on the new Baronet and in turn onto his son, if he could ever afford to have one.

Alena at eighteen was very lovely.

In fact 'beautiful' was most usually the word used to describe her.

She had sat silent whilst Mr. Lawson read out her father's will.

She now found that it was impossible to find words to express her feelings.

"I suppose," her brother asked after a long pause in which he had been thinking deeply, "I am not allowed to sell the house in London?"

"That too is entailed, Sir Robin, so I would suggest that you rent it out, but it is very large and since it has not been lived in for several years, it would require a great deal of restoration."

"Which, of course, I cannot afford."

Mr. Lawson nodded.

"And what about the estate?"

The Solicitor, who was a kindly man, sighed.

"I am afraid that two years ago your father sold the few hundred acres that were not entailed. The rest, like the garden, the stables and, of course, the private Racecourse, which are all in very bad repair, are also entailed."

Sir Robin and his sister had already been informed that the Dunstead Trustees, one of whom was Mr. Lawson himself, came round once a month to make sure everything was intact and in place.

What was really outstanding about Dunstead House was its magnificent collection of pictures that were always the envy of every art collector.

From where she was sitting now, Alena could see a picture by Rembrandt, another by Frans Hals and a third, which she had always especially loved, by Raphael.

It was his famous picture of *St. George and the Dragon*.

It passed dramatically through her mind now that if anyone had a dragon to fight it was her brother.

His dragon being the misery of complete poverty.

She looked up at the Raphael as she pondered their situation.

St. George mounted on his rearing white horse was not unlike Robin and the dragon with its long black wings and its snarling mouth appeared as horrifying as everything they had been told by Mr. Lawson.

As if he had nothing more to say and found it hard to control his feelings, Robin rose from his seat.

He walked to the mullion window and looked out at the garden.

He remembered it being perfectly kept with smooth green lawns and well kept flowerbeds.

He was not surprised that the lawns needed cutting and the flowerbeds appeared to have more weeds in them than flowers.

During his father's illness, the Solicitors, realising the family's dire financial position, had cut down the staff, so that in the house and on the estate there were as few men and women employed as possible.

Sir Robin had already discovered that the majority of the staff were old and they had been prepared to stay on for only a small wage because they had nowhere else to go.

But they were all far too old to keep the place in the perfect order he remembered from the days of his youth.

His father had been quite unable to communicate with anyone and he had therefore not come home earlier as he now thought he should have done.

The Viceroy had begged him, if it was possible, to stay on in India because of his excellent work, but he now realised that while he had wanted to stay, he should have returned home.

But even if he had, it would have been too late for him to stop the rot – far too late to prevent every penny his father possessed being squandered.

He most certainly had not expected that everything saleable would have been sold.

He could see now why there was an empty space on each side of the marble fireplace where there had been two exquisitely carved Queen Anne mirrors.

He had also noticed as soon as he came into the hall that the grandfather clock he had loved as a small child had disappeared.

There were spaces in the passage leading towards the reception rooms where there had once stood exquisite inlaid cabinets that every visitor admired.

Mr. Lawson had told Robin that he had drawn up a list of items that to his knowledge had been sold during the last five years.

He had pushed the dossier over the table, but Robin had not even looked at it.

'What is the point?' he thought to himself.

They had all gone and as there was little chance of their returning, it was a sheer waste of time regretting their disappearance.

What he needed to think about now was just how he and his sister could live without raising money with two large historic houses on their hands.

He was quite certain he would be blamed for letting matters deteriorate so far without knowing about it.

As he had not quizzed the Solicitors, they had been, as was correct, loyal to his father and no one had told him what was happening.

The late Baronet had always been an exceedingly generous man and he had never denied himself anything he really wanted.

He had bought the best horses and, as his friends commented mockingly, 'he lived like a Lord'.

There had always been a butler and six footmen at Dunstead Hall and it was very much the same in Dunstead House in Park Lane.

The magnificent collection of paintings had been started by the second Baronet and then added to by each of his successors.

The pictures were divided between the two houses and with walls groaning with such treasures, no one would believe that the present owner had no money to pay for his meals, let alone keep the two houses clean and tidy.

*

There was at the moment complete silence in the large study. It was where the late Baronet had always sat at his exquisite Regency writing table.

As Sir Robin did not turn from the window, Alena, who had been silent for some time, remarked,

"There must be something that we can do. But in the meantime, Mr. Lawson, you are quite right in thinking we would not like everyone to know about the predicament we are in."

"You can trust me, Miss Alena. I need not tell you of my deep affection for your family and, although it may seem presumptuous, I am very fond of this house because it contains more treasures than any other house I have ever visited."

"Treasures are certainly here, but I am wondering how we can keep them clean and from falling off the walls as even the cords that hang them need replacing."

Alena spoke as if she was very close to tears.

"I am certain," Mr. Lawson added, "that Sir Robin will find some way of making money. After all he bears a distinguished and ancient name and I am sure that there are many Companies that would welcome him as a director."

Robin turned round.

"I have been thinking of that. At the same time it would be a considerable disadvantage if they knew that the director who was there to help them in making money was himself completely penniless!"

"I agree with you," Mr. Lawson responded quickly. "That is why I have never breathed a word to anyone about your father's position, although I and my partners have for some months felt that something should be done."

"I think I should have been told much earlier, but we will not talk about it now. My father is dead and I have taken his place. Somehow I have to keep my sister and myself alive to preserve the contents of this house and the one in London."

"You could possibly," Mr. Lawson then suggested tentatively, "put the pictures into storage. Or loan them to one of our best museums."

"And make sure everyone is aware of our position! Of course I cannot do that. Besides the house itself, as you well know, is part of our British heritage."

Mr. Lawson made a helpless gesture with his hands but he did not say anything further.

"What I am going to ask you now is that you leave copies of my father's will for me and my sister and the list of everything that is entailed in both our houses, and as you have just promised, that you will on no account tell anyone of our present situation."

"I promise you, Sir Robin."

"We need to talk things over between ourselves and when we have come to a conclusion, we will contact you."

Realising that he was now dismissed, Mr. Lawson rose from the table saying,

"I can only offer you my deepest sympathy as well as my condolences and I assure you that I will help you in any way I possibly can."

There was a faint smile on his lips as he added,

"In fact, to be very practical, we will not send you a bill for our services during the last six months until you are in a position to pay it."

"I am most grateful," replied Robin.

He escorted Mr. Lawson to the door, shook him by the hand and left him to find his own way out.

He then turned to face his sister.

"*What* are we going to do, Alena? What the devil can we do?"

"I was just wondering the same, Robin, and in fact praying that we shall come up with some good ideas."

"I suppose," he asked, walking to the mantelpiece, "there is no point in looking round the house."

"After what Mr. Lawson has said, I should think it would a waste of time. I was just looking at this list he left us of the items that have been sold lately including most of the silver. I am quite certain that the George III tea-set will be entailed and so will the silver and gold plates."

Her brother sighed.

"It is no use making ourselves miserable looking at that list, Alena. What we have to do now is think of how we can make money and I suspect half the men in England are thinking the same at this very moment!"

"What quite a number of them are doing, especially

those with titles – as you have been abroad for so long you are not aware of it – is going to America and looking for an heiress."

Her brother stared at her.

"Looking for an heiress!"

"It has lately been the smart thing in New York for an American heiress to marry an Italian Prince, if one is available, or a French Duc."

"It makes me feel sick – in any case I suppose as a mere Baronet I would not qualify."

"The girls at school were very thrilled when Prince Colonna became engaged to an American heiress, and the newspapers in Florence reported that the list of American ladies marrying Italian Nobles was too long to be printed in one issue."

Robin laughed as Alena added,

"Your Baronetcy plus the pictures should count up to a million or two!"

"The whole idea horrifies me, Alena, but I did read in the Indian newspapers that Jennie Jerome, whoever she is, has married Lord Randolph Churchill."

"And Lord Craven, who I think Papa knew, married an American heiress."

"If you are insinuating I should be a fortune-hunter, I take it as a gross insult. I have no intention of marrying anyone and certainly not a woman who is only interested in my title."

Alena smiled at the violence in his voice but did not reply.

"If it comes to that, Alena, how about *you* marrying a millionaire? After all you are a very pretty girl and you are bound to receive many proposals and, if we are lucky, the man you accept could help us restore the two houses."

"He would already have a house of his own," Alena objected. "But, like you, I have no intention of marrying for money – only for love."

"I have an idea that love is going to be something neither of us can afford, but I have no intention of hawking my Baronetcy around in the hope that some American will take a fancy to it!"

"Seriously, Robin, we have to do something. We cannot just stay here and wait for the roof to fall in on our heads. And the same applies to the house in London.

"I drove past it today on my way here and thought how fine the old family home looked from the outside even though the windows were shuttered."

She drew in her breath.

"It is most unfair and I feel angry about it. Before I went off to Florence Papa promised he would give a ball for me when I became a *debutante* and that is exactly what I should be at this moment."

"Papa himself must have known even then that it was something he could not afford."

"I expect there was something still left in the house he could sell," Alena remarked practically. "There seem to be so many gaps on the walls now that he must have sold enough to give a dozen balls if I had been in England."

Robin threw himself down onto an armchair.

"If you are moaning about a ball you cannot have, I am feeling miserable that the stables are empty. When I was in India I used to dream of the Racecourse and how I enjoyed taking Papa's excellent horses over the jumps – I was always planning to build them higher and have even better bred horses when I took over the estate."

"I know exactly what you must be feeling," Alena sympathised, "and as I feel the same, we can cry together, but that is not going to do any good. We must be practical and find some way to preserve our heritage and especially the pictures."

She looked up at St. George striking the dragon.

She mused that if poverty was an enemy they could fight it like a living creature and it would make their lives so much easier.

"I suppose," Robin reflected, "that if we took one of these pictures abroad and sold it, we would be caught by the suspicious Trustees and doubtless convicted of theft."

"You can bet we would, Robin, and you heard Mr. Lawson state that the Trustees come round the two houses every month. A missing picture would be the first thing they would notice and they would make a big hue and cry."

She gave a laugh before she added,

"Don't forget that as Head of the family you cannot possibly allow a scandal of any sort."

"It would certainly be a huge scandal all right if we die of starvation!" Robin countered sarcastically.

Alena shrugged her shoulders.

"I expect there are some potatoes in the garden if nothing else."

Robin rose from the armchair.

"Damn it!" he exploded. "I am not going to die of starvation, nor am I going to sit here just thinking it a pity that our Papa has spent every penny we possessed. It was wrong and wicked of him, but you and I are not going to behave like nincompoops who don't even have the strength to save ourselves."

Alena clapped her hands.

"That's the way I like you to talk, Robin, and I feel quite certain you will find a solution of some kind."

There was silence until Robin exclaimed,

"I think I have an idea!"

"What can it be, Robin?"

"I am just working it out. But I would doubt if you will agree to it – "

"I'll agree to anything that improves our situation. And I'd prefer it to be something active. There is nothing worse than sitting and waiting for a calamity to strike one."

"I think this calamity has already struck us, Alena, and that is why I must do something positive – something that no one would expect."

"I agree, of course I do – but what is it?"

"I was just thinking," he began slowly, "that, when you talked about Englishmen with titles looking for a rich bride in America, they are going the wrong way about it."

"What do you mean?"

"Well, it is degrading for a man to sell his title and even more degrading to admit that he has to do so."

"Of course, that is true, Robin, but the Italians have cashed in on it and the English are now following them. I suspect all you can to do is to visit New York."

"I still say it's going the wrong way about it. What they should be doing is to stay here in England and make the American heiresses seek them."

"I don't know what you are talking about, Robin, and how can this idea of yours affect us?"

"What I am thinking is that now Papa has died and as I am the ninth Baronet, I would seem very romantic to a large number of women if I was also a rich man – with a magnificent house in London and a famous art collection known all over the world."

"That you most certainly have," agreed Alena, "but

the houses that hang the pictures are dilapidated, and your guests for dinner will hardly be amused to be served a poor menu with only water to drink!"

"That will not be the case if they come to England to meet me, or are here already, as I suspect some of them are. They will all come to Dunstead House in London and be received in the hall by the same number of liveried staff as there were when I was a boy.

"The *cuisine* will be just superb and the champagne sparkling. The host will be waiting for them to admire his pictures, his way of living and, of course, himself!"

"Well, that is a delightful daydream, Robin, but just like fairy gold it vanishes when you touch it! And who is going to pay for the footmen and the fine champagne?"

"That is the only snag, Alena. We must think how it can be done. Then I will open your Season in London by throwing a ball for you."

"I think you are raving mad. You could not afford to pay the orchestra nor could I afford to buy a new gown. Oh, Robin, do let's talk sense."

"I *am* talking sense," he insisted. "It is what I am intending to do, although first of all I have to think how I can somehow raise the money to be able to do it."

Alena stared at him.

"Are you really serious?"

"I am deadly serious. I have no intention of going around in rags and tatters and asking the rich folk that you and I have to marry to be sorry for us."

"So I come into it too!" exclaimed Alena.

"Of course you do, but you have to marry someone who can afford to keep you. And naturally he must be in love with you. In the meantime you are not going to have a proposal from anyone, even the dustman, down here."

He drew a deep breath and went on positively,

"We are going to London and we are going to open up the house. As your father's daughter a great number of people will be only too delighted to invite you to endless parties, where you will go suitably attired."

"And who is going to pay for my gowns?"

"*I am* – as soon as I can get hold of some money."

"And just how are you going to do so?"

"It is just a question of managing for a short time, then when we marry money, we can pay it all back."

"I still think the whole idea is mad, Robin. If, as I suspect, you are going to do something illegal to obtain the money, then we shall both end up, if not in prison, at least in disgrace. And no one will speak to us for the rest of our lives!"

She spoke very passionately and to her surprise her brother laughed.

"I was very certain that was what you would think, but you are wrong and you are going to do it all my way. I promise you that if we fail, it will be sheer stupidity on our part and not because we don't have the opportunity we are looking for."

"What opportunity, Robin?"

Her sank down beside her on the sofa and took her hand in his.

"Now listen to me, Alena, you and I are practical people. We have to face the fact that neither of us can live without money. *The only way is to marry it.*"

He paused before he added,

"But I am not crawling around kissing someone's feet because they are made of gold – and nor are you. If you do it my way, people will become interested in you, first because you are from a good family – "

He looked intently at Alena before he continued,

"They will all be bowled over when they see how beautiful you are, and lastly, although it will seem of little consequence, they will accept you as an equal because if they have money, you have it too."

"Very plausible, Robin, but quite impractical – "

"I don't think so and I just refuse to be a poor man tapping on the back door. If we fail we will go down in a cloud of glory, not just slip away humbly and grateful for any scraps that may fall from the rich man's table."

"That I admit would be very unpleasant, but I still cannot understand how we can possibly open the house in Park Lane or hold a ball for me."

"It is what you have been promised and it is what you are going to have. If we take risks together, it will not be as frightening as if we take them on our own."

"Risks! What risks?"

"I was just now wondering, dear Alena, whether I should tell you the truth or keep you in ignorance – "

"You cannot keep me in ignorance," she protested. "I suppose, however much I argue, I will do anything you think will help us out of this appalling and scary situation."

"That is just what it is. As I have already told you, we could easily crawl away and hide here in misery. I can shoot some rabbits and you can do the cooking. Everyone will be sorry for us, but will do little or nothing to help."

Alena shivered as she knew it was the truth.

If they stayed in this huge house with no servants, it was very doubtful whether any of their neighbours would be interested in them.

Certainly their so-called friends in London would take their names off their guest list.

"Now tell me the way out," she murmured.

"Well, what we are going to do is look around the house and find one of the least noticeable and, I suppose, least important of the famous pictures."

Alena gave a cry.

"You are *not* touching them. You know as well as I do that they are inspected by the Trustees every month and if you are thinking of selling one, they will come down on us like a ton of bricks."

"Not if I do it my way – "

"And what is your way then?"

"Strangely enough when I was sailing home in the ship from Calcutta there was a man on board – an Italian – who is a brilliant artist and to amuse the passengers he did some portraits of them and they were delighted."

"I am not surprised."

"When I talked to him, Alena, I found he had gone out to India not only to paint pictures which he could sell, but also to make replicas of one or two of the portraits of the first Viceroys that had been damaged by the heat and lack of proper attention.

"He showed me a copy of the portrait he had made of the first Viceroy, Lord Canning.

"I remember reading about him."

"I had to admit that the way he had copied it was brilliant. He was taking it back to England to be hung in the War Office and I swear that it would be impossible for anyone to know that it had not been painted by the original artist."

He could see Alena's eyes widening and continued,

"In addition he told me he had restored or rather reproduced one of William Pitt as Prime Minister. It had been damaged by the servants. When his reproduction was hung, it was impossible for anyone to know it was not the original painting."

"I can see what you are intending to do, but I am sure it is dangerous."

"Perhaps guessing instinctively what I was to find here, I asked my new friend, if I owned a picture that was extremely valuable and at the same time not publicly for sale, where would it be possible to dispose of it."

"I suppose he knew of someone?"

"He assured me he knew of where he could dispose of it perfectly safely.

"I cannot believe that if one of our pictures found its way into Europe, it would be easily traced if it appeared still to be hanging in its proper place and then no one could suspect it was not the original."

"It is a terrible risk," breathed Alena.

"I consider it more of a risk to sit here and wait to starve to death. I actually think it was fate that I had this conversation with the Italian and actually asked him before we parted if he would like to see our pictures in London.

"I was rather worried that he might copy one when we were not looking and we would be left with a substitute without being aware of it!"

"We must certainly not allow that to happen," said Alena, "and now that I think of it, most of our very best pictures are hanging in London. There are two Van Dycks for instance and I have always loved the one of Charles I."

"I like that one too and would hate to lose it."

"There is also the picture by Rembrandt that Papa was so fond of and I have always adored Boucher's *Cupid and the Graces*."

"I have no intention of letting that one out of my sight, but you and I, Alena, are aware that there are some attractive pictures in the collection that are so dirty from old age and neglect that no one would give them a second glance."

There was silence and then Alena asked,

"You really think this idea, which seems crazy to me, will work?"

"It has to. We cannot afford failure."

"I agree with you, but equally I am frightened that we are doing something wrong and will be found out."

"Actually if you think about it, Alena, whilst I am alive, everything belongs to me. Thus if anything is lost I am the loser and I cannot for the moment worry about my sons who are not yet born and are unlikely to be, unless I can provide them with a rich mother."

"That is one way of looking at it, but please, Robin, don't take any unnecessary risks."

"It is going to be one big risk anyway. I am driving to London tomorrow to find my friend and see how much money he can advance to me immediately so that we can open the house and start planning your debut."

Alena closed her eyes.

"I do *not* believe this is true, Robin, I think it is all a dream and when I wake up, we will find ourselves here with all the pictures crumbling on the walls and very dusty because we have no servants to clean them."

Robin bent forward and kissed her on the cheek.

"Nothing like that is going to happen. We are both Crusaders starting out to defend our rights and ultimately to be completely successful in finding all we seek."

"A rich wife and a rich husband," Alena remarked in a very small voice.

"And may they also be so fascinating that we fall in love with them!"

CHAPTER TWO

Alena spent a quiet day in the country after Robin had departed for London.

She walked round the overgrown garden and then spent a long time gazing at the pictures in the house.

She could not help feeling it was thrilling to own the work of so many famous artists, although the pictures all needed considerable attention.

But not one of them could help her and Robin.

She thought his idea of how they could provide for themselves was very risky and she almost hoped that when he reached London, he would not be able to find his friend.

Even if he did, he might well refuse to take part in anything beyond the law.

It was very quiet in the house and in the garden and she was still feeling somewhat miserable when she heard the sound of wheels outside in the drive.

This meant that Robin had returned.

One of the farmers had taken him to the Station and she suspected that he had somehow found a lift back.

She ran out to meet him as he reached the top of the steps outside the front door.

"I am back," he announced unnecessarily.

"I can see you are, Robin, I have been counting the hours that have passed very slowly, until I saw you again. Come into the sitting room. I thought it would be too late for tea, but there is a cool drink and a sandwich if you are hungry."

"Actually, my friend Luigi gave me an excellent luncheon – and everything is satisfactory."

Alena gave a little cry.

"That is just what I was waiting to hear. You really mean he will do as you suggested?"

"He has started already!"

"What do you mean?"

"I met him at eleven o'clock and took him straight to the house in Park Lane."

"Was there anyone there, Robin?"

"No one. The house was all shut up, but of course I had taken a set of keys with me. If there was meant to be a caretaker, there was no sign of one."

"I should have thought that was very dangerous."

"I thought the same, but everything was intact and I have now arranged for a caretaker to start tomorrow."

"Of course we will need a large number of servants if we do move in," Alena murmured under her breath.

"Now let me start from the beginning, Alena – "

He drank some lemonade that Alena had made for him and began,

"I told Luigi just what we required. As I told you, copying is something he is a great expert at. He agreed to do what I asked and we drove immediately to Park Lane."

Alena was listening and holding her breath as she just could not believe that Robin's extraordinary plan could really be put into action.

"As we both expected the house is dusty inside and somewhat dilapidated, but not really as bad as I expected."

"Well, that's a relief!" she exclaimed.

"It will surely save time, which is more important than money."

Alena wondered why, but did not want to interrupt him with too many questions.

"Luigi walked down the Picture Gallery and I knew he was thrilled by the pictures. He was particularly excited by the Bouchers and the Gainsboroughs.

Alena gave a little cry.

"Oh, I am sure they are too well known. Everyone who paid a visit to the house in the old days praised our Gainsboroughs, the Vandykes and the Rembrandts."

"Luigi is sharp enough to realise that. Therefore he chose two of our oldest pictures that he thought would not be as well known, even by art experts, as those you have just mentioned."

"Which ones are they?"

"Perhaps it will surprise you, but one was *St. Mary Magdalene with a Candle* by La Tour, which was painted somewhere between 1630 and 1635."

Alena was looking surprised.

She could recall this picture because she had never thought it particularly attractive.

At the same time she was knowledgeable enough to know that in the seventeenth century there had been great devotion to Mary Magdalene in all Catholic countries.

She could remember her father telling her that the Saint's beauty had made her more appealing to members of the Church because of her repentance.

The picture itself, Alena remembered, was not one of her favourites.

The Saint's body was all enveloped in a mysterious darkness and only parts of her face were illuminated by the candle.

Now she thought of it, she remembered as a child noticing some books on the table by the candle.

There was also a wooden cross and a scourge which was bloodstained, but Alena had not understood at the time that this was part of Mary Magdalene's penitence.

When she grew older she had turned away from the picture, feeling it was rather unpleasant.

As if Robin was reading her thoughts, he remarked,

"I can understand you not being particularly fond of that picture. Luigi told me that he had heard it suggested that La Tour used a gypsy as his model. There were many in Lorraine at that time."

"Do you really think that your friend can copy this picture so perfectly that no one will ever discover that the original has been removed?" Alena asked him hesitantly.

"I have seen some of his work, and I defy anyone to form any suspicion that the picture they are looking at was not painted by the artist who had signed it."

Alena did not want to speak and he continued,

"What is so clever is that Luigi has collected over the years a large number of old canvases of various ages. Therefore our copy of Mary Magdalene will be painted on a seventeenth century canvas that would, I am very certain, convince an expert it had been painted in that century."

"It certainly all sounds exceedingly clever, Robin, and what was his second choice?"

"That will be a surprise to you as much as it was a surprise to me – "

He paused almost theatrically.

"He next chose, *Portrait of a man – Il Condottiere*, which was painted by Antonello da Messina in 1475."

Alena wrinkled her forehead.

"I don't think I can remember that picture. Is it the only one we have by that artist?"

"The only one – and perhaps you will remember it more easily when I tell you it is still on its original panel of poplar wood."

Alena gave a cry.

"Of course. It is another picture I never liked and therefore never bothered with it. The head of a rather ugly, frightening-looking man."

"Exactly, Alena. He was supposed, Luigi thinks, to express the proud commanding spirit characteristic of the early Renaissance."

Alena was recalling the clenched jaw and the stern expression on the face.

Her father had said the scar on his upper lip showed he might have been a military leader and that was why he was nicknamed *Il Condottiere*.

"I really don't mind you taking that one, Robin, but surely, if it is on wood, it will be much more difficult than if Luigi was painting on canvas."

"Actually he said it was helpful. He has a panel of poplar wood and the background, the cap and the clothing have darkened so whilst the face stands out dramatically, there is less painting required for the rest of it than in any other picture he might have chosen."

"I see his point – and quite frankly he is welcome to that picture!"

"Very welcome indeed and then you will next hear what he expects to receive for the two pictures."

"What is he going to get? I have forgotten that he is going to sell them for us. But surely that is dangerous, since people will ask where the pictures have come from."

"Not as dangerous as it may sound – for the simple

reason that Luigi has a dedicated patron who is building up a magnificent collection of paintings of originals that he wishes to keep secret, and what is more he trusts Luigi and will not ask awkward questions."

"*A secret collection!* I just cannot believe it, Robin. Would not any man who owns so many beautiful pictures like ours want to boast about them?"

"Apparently Luigi's patron, and incidentally he is a French Duc and obscenely rich, has no intention of sharing his prized pictures with anyone. They are locked up in his château, and according to Luigi, he sits staring at them day after day and asks nothing more from the world."

"He sounds a little mad, but I suppose we should be grateful as it is to our advantage."

"Very much to our advantage, Alena, and what do you imagine Luigi has advanced me already for these two pictures? And he is quite certain that when the Duc sees them, there will be more to come."

"How much?"

"Two thousand pounds."

Alena stared at him.

"I just don't believe it!"

"It's true," he insisted, "and as Luigi had the money with him I took it at once to the Bank."

"That was certainly very sensible of you, Robin, it would be ghastly if it was stolen."

"It is going to supply us with everything we need at present. Thus I want you to come to London tomorrow. We will move into the house secretly and not announce our arrival to the Social world until we have made sure that the house is more or less shipshape."

"Is there really very much to do to it, Robin?"

"Not as much as I feared. The walls are intact and

the ceilings have not fallen in. I feel a number of servants working hard would soon make a great deal of difference.

"I am leaving the curtains to you, Alena, as I expect they will need replacing. New cushions and flowers and candles in shining chandeliers will work wonders!"

Alena clasped her hands together.

"So it really is true!" she cried. "You are quite sure that what Luigi gave you is not fairy gold?"

"If it is, that is the Bank's responsibility. I am quite certain that from now on we are sitting on a gold mine!"

"But you must not sell any more pictures," Alena exclaimed. "You know if you are greedy it always means disaster."

"I am not greedy, but I am only too well aware how long that money has to last us. Long enough in fact to find me an amiable and rich wife and for you a millionaire!"

Alena laughed.

"That is most definitely unlikely."

"With your face he should be a *multi*-millionaire, but I suspect there are very few of them about."

Now they were both laughing.

Alena placed her arms round her brother's neck and kissed him on his cheek.

"You have so been brilliant, Robin. I thought when you told me what you were going to do, it was impossible. But now it has actually happened, I can only say that you are very much cleverer than I thought you could ever be!"

Robin chuckled.

"The copies of the pictures have yet to be made, but in the meantime, just in case any of those nosey Trustees start looking round, Luigi has been very astute."

"In what way?"

"He brought with him a seventeenth century canvas with a picture on it so damaged that it would be difficult for anyone to decipher what the subject of the painting had originally been."

"So it is hanging in the Picture Gallery now?"

"Exactly, and Luigi has promised me that a wooden panel in the same state of dilapidation will be in the frame of the da Messina by tonight."

Alena gave a sigh of relief.

"I cannot believe that the Trustees will be creeping around without us knowing it, but frankly I trust no one."

"That is very sensible and it means that no one but ourselves and Luigi must ever know what has happened this afternoon in Dunstead House."

Robin looked round him.

"Perhaps one day we will be able to afford to repair this house, but at present we have to concentrate on the one in Park Lane,"

"Yes, or course, Robin."

"We will not be extravagant," he carried on, as if he was thinking it out for himself. "At the same time I want to make a show. What you have to do as soon as you have packed your bag is to make a list of everyone you can think of who could be invited to your *debutante* ball."

"I have Mama's address book somewhere and that will give us the names of her friends she entertained in the past, and they will at least know who we are, even though they have not seen us for years."

"And I will make a list of the friends I had before I went to India and those I have seen since. Even if they do not come to our ball, they will know we exist, and that, for the moment is important."

"Now what about clothes?" enquired Alena.

"You can buy all you think absolutely necessary, but they must look costly and fashionable and as if you had thousands of others waiting for you to wear them."

Alena laughed.

"That will be the day! And naturally, dear Robin, I will be as careful as possible not to be extravagant."

"Equally Alena, your clothes must look spectacular. Remember that we are pretending to be as rich as Papa was before he threw his money away in that idiotic manner!"

He thought for a moment and then added,

"As he had been so ill, most people will remember Papa when he had the best horses and gave most amusing parties. Therefore they will not be the least surprised if we do the same."

"Horses! Can we really afford any horses?" Alena asked breathlessly.

"We will have two to ride in Rotten Row with the smartest team ever known to draw a carriage. It is what is expected of a rich man and naturally I will be talking about all the racehorses I intend to buy later in the Season when I have had a chance to look round at what is available."

"I have never asked before, Robin, because I forgot about it, but what happened to Papa's horses that were kept at Newmarket?"

"I asked that as soon as I returned. He sold them all lock stock and barrel with the stables thrown in."

"He must have received a good sum for them."

"It did not last him long," Robin replied caustically.

Now there was a hard note in his voice and Alena had heard it whenever he referred to his father. She could understand how bitter he felt at the way the family fortune had been dissipated.

To change the subject, she said quickly,

"Now you must decide how many servants we will need in Park Lane. I remember the Agency Mama went to when she wanted a new housekeeper. You recall that Mrs. Dodson has died."

"That's a great pity. She would have organised all this very easily without turning a hair."

His sister smiled.

"She would have been ninety by now, and I doubt if she would have been as efficient as you would wish."

"I forget people grow old and it will happen to us if we do not hurry up and get on with our lives!"

"We are really doing our best, Robin, and you have certainly been brilliant in finding this Italian man."

"I never thought that when he talked so eagerly to me on the ship about Papa's collection, which of course he had heard of, that he would come in so useful. He in fact was astonished when I told him what I required."

"But he agreed – "

"At once and with enthusiasm."

But all Alena could think about was that her prayers had been answered and although perhaps God had helped them in some strange way, at least they did not have to sit around and do nothing.

"What are you going to do about this house now?" Alena asked him.

"I will give the two old dears who are looking after us enough money to make them fat and happy. We cannot do everything all at once and Dunstead Hall in the country will have to wait until we have found our millionaires."

Alena wanted to ask him what would happen if the millionaires never turned up and then she told herself she must not think negatively.

She just had to believe that this desperate effort of Robin's would succeed.

And that somehow by a miracle they could each be married not just to a very rich spouse but to one who really loved them.

'Please God, please make it happen,' she prayed in her heart.

She continued praying as she went upstairs to pack the few clothes she was taking with her to London.

*

They set off very early the next morning, catching what was called the 'milk train', because it was the train on which the farmers sent their fresh milk up to the City.

They travelled by third class and Robin said firmly that it would be for the last time.

When they reached Paddington Station, they took a Hackney carriage to Dunstead House in Park Lane.

He opened the door and Alena entered nervously.

She found that the large hall with its long windows was not in as bad a condition as she had expected, although the Greek Gods in the alcoves were thick with dust.

The great fireplace had not been cleaned out since there had last been a fire in it.

In the huge chandelier hanging from the ceiling the candles had burnt themselves out leaving black grease.

But there was no real damage.

They walked silently from the hall into the study – the room the family always used when they were alone, as the vast drawing room and the reception rooms on the first floor were kept for formal parties.

When Alena had last seen the house, it had seemed to her surprisingly pretty.

But now the blue curtains needed cleaning and the white panelled walls were dirty but not badly cracked.

The shelf of the exquisitely carved mantelpiece had been covered with beautiful pieces of china, but there was nothing on it now, not even the old clock ornamented with Dresden porcelain that Alena recalled so well.

She supposed they had all been sold.

The large collection of family miniatures was still hanging on one side of the fireplace.

Robin pulled back the curtains and opened up the shutters and now Alena could see the famous collection of snuff boxes – some of the more ornate and bejewelled ones were missing.

What was most important was that all the pictures were intact.

They were mostly by French artists like Boucher and Nicholas Lancets, each one priceless in itself and they seemed to smile at them.

Alena thought that they would still impress, as they always had, anyone who visited the house.

Robin was watching her and as she turned to look at him, he enquired,

"Well, what is your verdict?"

"It might be a lot worse and it would not cost much to buy new curtains and covers."

"I think you will say the same of the drawing room, Alena, but the ballroom is a real mess."

They went to inspect it, but in fact Alena was not as despondent as her brother.

The walls needed repainting and much of the glass in the tall windows opening into the garden was broken, but, as she pointed out, the ceiling was intact and the dance floor undamaged.

"Again I can only say it might be worse, Robin."

"Alright, Alena, we will carry out your orders here and I will see to the stables and more vital than anything else, the kitchen."

"We cannot acquire the reputation of having a dirty kitchen!"

She was rather appalled when she saw it.

Obviously the last servants working in the kitchen when the Baronet was ill had done little or nothing but feed themselves.

The floor was filthy and the walls were almost as bad. Most of the chairs were broken and there seemed to be an extraordinary shortage of pots and pans.

"They must have been a slovenly set of servants," Alena asserted sourly, "and I think they stole everything they could get away with."

And this included the cutlery, although all the silver had been checked by the Trustees.

Robin looked round and commented,

"Now I am going to talk to a firm to undertake the restoration of the house. Luigi has given me the name of one he recommends. They were working on the last house he visited that belongs to someone most distinguished."

He smiled before he added,

"Naturally he would not confide in me the name of his client any more than he would reveal mine."

"That at least is honest and I only hope he does not blackmail you."

"I don't think it will be worth his while. His patron the Duc gives him any money he requires to purchase the pictures he is collecting for him, and being an Italian I am sure a considerable amount of it goes into his own pocket."

"Which is only fair – "

"Exactly!"

He left Alena and she went into the dining room, a most impressive room that could seat fifty or sixty people without any difficulty.

The tables needed polishing and the fireplace was as dirty as the others, but the furniture was outstanding.

She knew that if the room was cleaned and properly lit, it would be as beautiful again as when she was a child.

Alena had been sensible enough to bring some food with her and now she set it out on the table.

Then on an impulse she found a key in the pantry that she thought must belong to the cellar.

She went down the stone steps, remembering how frightening the cellar had seemed when she was small.

Her father had sometimes taken her with him when he was choosing which wine he would drink at dinner.

Now as she opened the door it was not surprising to see that the cellar appeared empty – there were only empty bins where the wine had once lain.

Then she remembered that there was another cellar further on – it was fitted with a special lock that her father had invented and did not require a key.

He had shown her how to work the lock, telling her that it was a deep secret so that the servants could not steal from him.

There was a good chance, Alena reckoned, that the lock was still effective.

She twisted the dial just as her father had shown her and to her delight the door opened.

When she looked inside, she saw that there was at least two dozen bottles each of claret, champagne and port.

She picked up one of the bottles of champagne and closed the door of the cellar behind her.

She hurried upstairs to the kitchen and as there was no ice, she stood the champagne in a bucket of cold water.

Then she waited for Robin's return.

It was approaching two o'clock before he appeared and by that time she was feeling hungry.

She heard him open the front door and ran into the hall.

"I thought you were lost!" she cried.

"I have come back with good news, my dear sister, and I am feeling ravenous."

"Luncheon is now served, my Lord," Alena intoned mockingly, "but before I tell you my news that will please you, I want to know what has happened."

"I have now arranged everything," Robin replied as he put down his hat on a chair. "The men will be arriving at dawn tomorrow morning and they have promised me I will have their best workmen and everything will be done at express speed."

"That is splendid news, Robin. Now because you have been a good boy, you shall have your reward. A glass of champagne!"

"*Champagne*! Where did it come from?"

"I remembered Papa's secret way into the back of the cellar and there are sufficient bottles there to keep you happy until the show begins."

Robin chuckled.

"The show is going to begin sooner than I expected. You must sit down tonight and write your invitations to the ball which will take place in exactly two weeks time."

Alena stared at him.

"Are you quite certain it is now possible?"

"Absolutely certain, Alena. The man I went to see knows the house. In fact he has worked here in the past. I told him that it was dilapidated as I had been abroad and, as I do not want you to miss the Season, I would employ a firm that would work the quickest and make it possible for your ball to take place before the end of May."

"And he agreed?"

"He jumped at it. I explained that the house was in a bad state because my father had been ill for over a year, and he understood. It was not because I could not afford to spend money on it."

"Will he be very expensive?"

"I told him that if he was successful here, I had a house in the country that was in a far worse state, but I was not going to place it anyone's hands until I had seen what he could do for me."

"That was very astute of you, Robin."

"He is going to do his best as cheaply as possible, and that is exactly what we need."

"I think you really do deserve a glass of champagne and I hope it will be cool enough."

Alena ran to the kitchen to fetch it for him.

As she did so she thought how fortunate they were and so far everything seemed to be going so smoothly and without too many difficulties.

Once again she was praying that God would help them and that nothing would go wrong.

'Please, God, please,' she murmured as she carried the champagne into the dining room, 'make Robin happy. He is trying so very hard and it would break his heart if he failed.'

When luncheon was over Alena did as Robin had told her.

She sat down at the writing table that her mother had always used and with the address book in front of her, she copied out the names and addresses of everyone in it.

There were a large number and when Robin came back, she asked him,

"Just how many invitations have you ordered to be printed? I have written nearly four hundred envelopes."

"Five hundred actually and some will be unable to come. Some may even be dead, but at least they will know we have arrived and are back on the stage!"

Alena smiled at him.

"Very much so, Robin, and if the drama turns out as you expect, they will all want to come."

"They will *all* come, but what we have to do is to make our party somehow unlike anyone else's."

"What do you mean, Robin?"

"Everyone gives a ball for a *debutante*, but you are different. You are prettier than the average boring girl and I want you to do something that people will find amusing, exciting and unusual and will always remember it."

Alena threw up her hands.

"You are asking far too much. What can I do short of walking in on my hands on the ceiling?"

"I have thought of that, but it's not good enough! We must think of something that no one has done before, and which will be the talk not only of London but of other countries including America."

"If *you* are still contemplating an American," Alena stated, "I can tell you here and now I have no intention of marrying an American!"

He did not say anything so she continued,

"There were two American girls at the school in Florence, and I thought their brothers, when they called to see them, were very boring and did not seem in the least significant. Also the stories the girls told of what goes on in New York made me very glad I am British."

"Of course it did, Alena, but sadly the British at the moment are not particularly famous for their wealth, while American riches are increasing year by year."

He made a gesture with his hands.

"It was only just a few days ago that yet more oil wells were found in Dallas and the Yanks are indeed miles ahead of us British in their invention of new machinery, mechanical instruments and photography."

"I do suppose you are right, Robin, but that does not make their people more attractive."

"Give them a chance. They are a young nation and that is why they have been clever enough to learn from us. Sooner or later they will not only produce what we need, but they will become more civilised in our eyes."

It was quite a speech and Alena clapped her hands.

"Then three cheers for the U.S.A!" she cried, "but you must forgive me if I prefer England and the English gentleman."

"In which case I only hope he has something in his pocket," Robin added sarcastically. "If you let him marry you thinking that you hold the cash, I have a feeling your marriage will not be as blissful as you hope."

Alena did not answer him as there was nothing she could say.

She knew that, if she deceived an Englishman by pretending to be a rich woman when she was penniless, he would never forgive her.

Therefore unless she could meet someone who was different in every way, she would have to do what Robin had told her to do – and that was to marry an American or perhaps a wealthy European.

Then she remembered that the French and Italians, if they were anyone of importance, always had arranged marriages and she had heard her friends at school talking about it.

One of them had remarked wistfully,

"I hope I will be able to choose my own husband, but Papa already has someone in mind whose family is just as aristocratic as ours and who thus will have his marriage arranged for him as soon as he becomes of age."

"Surely it must be so frightening," Alena had said, "to have to marry someone because your father approves of him while you may think him horrible!"

The girl she was talking to had smiled.

"Papa loves me and I love him, so I know he will not choose someone who is repulsive. At the same time as our family goes back to the twelfth century, I can hardly have a husband who cannot also boast of his blue blood."

Alena had no answer to this, but she thought then as she believed now that to marry any man without love, whoever he was, was wrong.

Yet she had to tell herself she had no alternative.

As Robin had said, they either had to sit down and starve or find someone who could keep them in the manner their father and mother had been accustomed to before all the money was spent.

As if he knew what she was thinking, he bent down and kissed her.

"Do stop worrying, dearest, luck is on our side and, who knows, the God of Love himself – Apollo – may drop down from Heaven and ask you to be his wife!"

CHAPTER THREE

Alena cooked breakfast for her brother and he then rushed off saying he had an idea about the servants.

"I was thinking of going to the Agency," Alena had said.

"You can go this afternoon if I fail, but I have an idea that I know will please you if it comes off."

He would not say anymore to her, but left his sister curious as he hurried out of the house.

Already the men from the firm Robin had engaged to begin the restoration of the house had arrived.

Alena insisted that they worked on the kitchen first.

"I absolutely refuse," she thundered, "to cook any more in that dirty place. It only wants soap and water to make it usable even if it is not very pretty."

"It must all be renovated properly," Robin agreed, "otherwise the servants we employ will not think it good enough for them."

Alena laughed.

"I will believe it when I see it. At present the only person you have to do everything is *me*."

"And you do it very well," he conceded, "but I have other ideas where you are concerned."

He hurried away and she smiled as she washed up the cups and plates they had used for breakfast.

Then she went into the study and sat down again at her mother's writing table.

First she took a long look at St. George killing the dragon and told him that he should help her in her task that was just as difficult as his.

Robin had not yet decided the exact date of the ball, so there was no point in her writing out the invitations that anyway ought to be printed or typed.

"I think actually," he had said, "it might be more effective in the case of Mama's friends if you put a little note inside. They would then feel obliged to help as Mama is dead – and sympathy and cooperation is something we need very badly at this moment."

"Very well, I will do as you suggest," she agreed.

She thought when he left her that what she could do now was to write the same letter to everyone in Robin's name, explaining that he was giving the ball for his sister Alena, 'as having been in mourning and in the country for so long, I want her to meet her parents' old friends'.

'I think that will sound rather pathetic,' Alena said to herself as she wrote out the letter for Robin to approve. 'We certainly need all the kindness we can get!'

It was nearly one o'clock when Robin came back.

He burst into the room telling her before he spoke that he brought exciting news.

"I have done it! I have done it!" he cried. "And I know you will be delighted, Alena."

"Done what?"

"I have engaged Burley to come back as butler!"

Alena looked at him blankly.

"Burley?"

"You surely must remember him. He was with us as a footman for years. He became the butler when Papa was taken ill and stayed until the Solicitors sacked him."

"Oh, of course!" Alena exclaimed. "But I did not remember his name."

"I suddenly recalled when I asked about him that he had gone on to White's Club. I went there this morning to find he was one of the Stewards."

"And he is coming back to us?"

"He is delighted to do so and I have told him what he is expected to do. That is to engage all the servants we require and there are to be quite a lot of them."

"It will be lovely to have someone who has known us before, Robin. How clever of you to think of him!"

"I have been clever in another way as well," Robin added smugly, "and this came to me in a flash."

"Now what can that be?" asked Alena.

"I was thinking about the ball and that, as the men are working only in the kitchen at the moment, it is going to take quite a long time before they start work on the front of the house and the ballroom."

Alena shrugged her shoulders.

"I am afraid that is inevitable."

"Which would mean we would have to put off your ball until the end of the Season, instead of giving it at once so that you will be invited to all the other balls."

"Naturally, but it cannot be helped."

"Yes it can, if you do what I want you to do."

Alena looked mystified.

"You will invite all the guests in two weeks time to a *Moonlight Ball*."

She stared at him.

"A Moonlight Ball?" she repeated.

"I was wondering what we could do that would be original and then suddenly this came to mind. We can use the new form of electric lighting in the main rooms and the ballroom."

Alena gave a gasp as Robin continued,

"But we shall not have time to install it completely. There will be just enough to create a huge moon that will throw a silvery light in the ballroom."

Alena clapped her hands together.

"It's a brilliant idea, Robin, what you are saying is that the guests will not see the dilapidated state of the walls and the pillars."

"That is the idea and if there are plenty of flowers, the place will look amazingly beautiful."

He smiled before he added,

"And, of course, you must wear a gown that glitters like moonlight."

"You are so clever, Robin, that it is a great pity you cannot sell your brilliant ideas and make a fortune."

"I promise you, Alena, that our Moonlight Ball will be a huge success. I shall also have a moon in the dining room and smaller ones in the hall and passages."

Alena could not help feeling excited.

She had been thinking that, unless they could hurry up the workmen, no one was going to be at all impressed by the house, only by the Picture Gallery.

Now she thought that if Burley produced enough housemaids they could easily clean away all the dust and polish the furniture.

It would be very difficult for anyone in the artificial moonlight to notice that the carpet was shabby and the sofa and chairs needed re-covering.

Robin was delighted with his ideas and talked about them all through luncheon and was hardly aware of what he was eating.

Alena had realised that they would not be able to eat in the kitchen, so she had asked one of the workmen to buy some food in Shepherds Market.

She had made a list for him of meat and fruit, a loaf of bread and a large packet of butter and she hoped that Robin would think it sufficient.

As it was he ate everything, drank some claret she had brought up from the cellar and hurried off.

He said he had so much to do and Alena did not ask for details as she thought it would delay him.

She began writing out copies of Robin's letter.

She was now feeling so much more optimistic than she had earlier in the day.

*

It was a sheer delight when Burley arrived.

He was obviously as excited at coming back to the house as Alena and Robin were at having him.

"I miss the house in the country, Miss Alena," he said, "but it weren't the same when Sir Edward became so ill. There be no one then to wait on them nurses who all complained at everything I did for them."

"Oh, I don't believe it, Burley. We always thought you were perfect."

Burley laughed.

"That's just what I missed when you'd gone, Miss Alena."

"Well, I hear Sir Robin has given you a free hand, Burley, so please find us plenty of good and hard-working housemaids. You can see the mess this house is in."

"I'm not surprised as it's been empty for so long, but I'll soon make it shipshape. Don't you and Sir Robin worry. Just leave it to me."

He went off to visit the Agency and as Alena was to find our later, he got in touch with some of his friends, who were only too pleased to join him.

Alena realised that, of course, Robin had let Burley think that money was no object.

Now their father was dead everything that had gone wrong during his illness had to be forgotten.

"I was always afraid you'd not be able to open this house, Sir Robin," Burley commented.

Knowing he was very curious, Robin replied,

"I have come into some money I did not expect. So I can now see Miss Alena has a proper 'coming-out' as a *debutante* – and that is why we must be in London."

"Yes, Sir Robin, I can understand."

Burley certainly did not skimp in engaging the staff they required.

Fortunately there was enough livery upstairs in the attic to house the four footmen who would be on duty in the hall.

There were two pantry boys cleaning the silver, as well as a scullion and two assistants for the cook.

It was indeed fortunate, Burley remarked, that his older sister had been widowed the previous year and would like to come back into service.

She had been the head housemaid to a distinguished Nobleman and therefore the position of housekeeper over six young maids was very much to her liking.

It was a joy, Alena thought, to retire to bed so soon after their arrival and find everything prepared – her bed turned down and her nightgown laid out.

Hot water was in a brass can on the washstand and the dust in the room had disappeared as if by a magic hand.

Robin had naturally taken the Master bedroom and Burley was valeting him until he could find someone, who in his words, was 'up to his job'.

"I am so happy with you here, Burley," Robin had said quietly.

"That's as maybe, Sir Robin, but when things get busy, I can't attend to your clothes in the way I'd want and have the dining room up to scratch as well. I'll find a valet, but he's got to be someone I've complete confidence in."

Robin smiled as Burley was certainly proving his worth.

"It was brilliant of you to think of him," Alena said again the evening after he had arrived.

Robin had other news that he thought fantastic.

"I have just called in at the American Embassy," he boasted when he came home late for tea.

"Why did you go there?" Alena asked him.

"You know the answer. I was wondering how we could make the Americans aware of us as much as we are so aware of them."

"You cannot be serious about both of us marrying Americans," Alena remarked nervously.

"It is where the money is, Alena, and that, as you are well aware, is exactly what we need – "

There was a pause before he added,

"And as quickly as possible!"

Alena knew he was telling her that even the large amount of money they had received from the Italian artist was not going to last for ever.

She therefore waited curiously and apprehensively for him to tell her what he had achieved at the Embassy.

"I introduced myself to the American Ambassador and told him I was a huge admirer of the strides America was making, especially in shipbuilding and modern design of machinery.

"I hope he was impressed by your remarks."

"He was indeed and I said I was thinking of going to America shortly myself as I was contemplating buying a yacht!"

Alena stared in surprise at him as he went on,

"I could think of no one who could provide me with one that was more up-to-date and had all the latest gadgets than the American firm which has already produced some sailing ships that are far more advanced than ours."

"He must have enjoyed all that flattery!"

"He was very delighted, especially as I implied that I would be sparing no expense on any yacht I purchased."

Alena laughed because it all seemed so ridiculous.

"I then invited him and his wife to our ball and said I would be sending him an invitation in the next two days."

"I am sure he accepted with alacrity."

"He certainly did and I then asked him if there were any young and pretty American girls in London at present. I thought it would be nice for you, when you come with me to New York to have some friends there already."

Alena laughed.

"Oh, Robin, you are too sharp for words!"

"I rather thought so myself too, especially after the Ambassador gave me *this* list!"

He drew some papers from his pocket and put them down in front of his sister.

Alena saw that there were two pages of names and addresses.

"Things are certainly moving quickly, Robin, but I am afraid if we go too fast we shall make mistakes."

"The faster the better. We must get this ball going first. You will see that one of the girls named here comes from one of the richest families in the whole of the U.S.A."

Alena looked down and saw the name Mary-Lee Vanderhart.

"Is that her?" she asked.

"Yes. According to the newspapers she is worth, or rather her father is, two or three hundred million with even more to come!"

"Well, it ought to take you some time to spend that amount! But it would be such a great mistake to count your chickens before they are hatched."

"I am well aware of that, Alena. The newspapers have also told me that she is very beautiful."

There was a pause and then Alena commented,

"I am certain that anyone with that money would be described as beautiful even if she had a face like the back of a cab!"

"Now you are being cynical and you, my dearest, will not only be far more beautiful than any of your guests, but will appear to have more money than any of them!"

Alena laughed.

"I think this daydream of yours is gradually turning into a circus, Robin, and I am quite certain the clowns will appear soon!"

"The only clowns here will be us if we make fools of ourselves, Alena. This is our one big opportunity and I assure you I am not going to make a mess of it."

As he spoke there was a loud crash in the corridor outside and he hurried out to see what had happened.

Alena thought it was merely one of the workmen who had dropped a ladder or perhaps his tools.

So she sat down at her writing table again and then she looked at the list Robin had given her and shuddered.

It was all very well to talk lightly of marrying a rich American for his money, but after all she was indeed the same flesh and blood as they were.

Once she and Robin were married there would be no escape.

'I don't want to think about it,' Alena told herself.

As she was writing the additional envelopes and the letters which Robin had to sign, it was difficult not to feel she was plunging deeper and deeper into a quagmire that might eventually engulf her completely.

It was late that evening when Alena rose from the writing table with a sigh.

She had been working at the invitations all day and it was not as easy as it had appeared at first.

She had to make sure that her mother's and father's friends were still alive.

Although there was a *Debrett's* in the house, it was out of date and she thought that tomorrow she must make Robin buy or borrow a new one.

She now had written out invitations for nearly five hundred people and if only half of them accepted it would still be a large ball.

She hoped that Burley would have engaged a cook by this evening, although he did say he had an excellent chef coming the following morning and in the meantime he would cook anything Alena required himself.

*

Robin decided to go to his Club.

"I shall meet friends there who will be delighted to be asked to the ball and I would like to know if some of the

Officers who served with me in the Regiment are still at Knightsbridge Barracks."

He left at seven o'clock and Alena had eaten alone.

Burley felt that the enormous dining room that was not yet properly cleaned would be somewhat depressing.

Instead he brought her dinner on a tray to the study and she found that the supper he had prepared for her was delicious.

It made her feel strong enough to go on until she had finished the task her brother had set for her, but it had taken her far longer than she thought it would.

When she glanced at the clock she saw that it was nearly midnight – and that meant that Burley would have locked the front door and gone to bed.

"We might engage a nightwatchman later," he had said, "but your father, Miss Alena, was always against our keeping a footman up all night and I'm sure you'll agree it's unnecessary."

"When you think just how long the house has been empty, it's so amazing it has not been burgled. But I don't think we need worry."

"I'll get everything just perfect at soon as possible," Burley promised. "But it all takes time."

"Of course it does, Burley, and I do think you have done wonders already."

"As Sir Robin kindly keeps saying, but this be only the beginning and we've a long way to go yet."

When Burley said goodnight, he told Alena that he had put an oil lamp in the hall so that Robin would see his way when he returned and the candles had been lit in her bedroom.

They were using lamps and candles although Robin kept talking about electric light.

Alena put down her pen – her fingers were aching after the length of time she had been writing.

Then she stretched out her arms and yawned.

'If I don't retire to my bed soon,' she thought, 'I shall be late in the morning.'

She blew out the five candles intending to grope her way to the door.

Just as she was about to do so, she heard a slight sound outside the window.

No one had drawn the curtains and she had thought it rather pleasant when she looked up from her work to see the moonlight in the garden at the back of the house.

The garden itself certainly needed much attention, but it was no use thinking about gardeners until they had engaged everyone they needed in the house.

Alena thought the most sensible thing would be to find a firm to restore the garden as it had been originally with a neat lawn, flower beds and comfortable seats under the trees.

There was also a fountain, but she was sure it had not worked for a very long time and she knew that it was a luxury she must not ask for at the moment.

Now as she looked towards the window, she saw to her astonishment that there was a man outside.

She wondered who it could possibly be.

Perhaps it was Burley looking to see if she had shut and locked the windows before she retired to bed.

Before she could decide if it was he or perhaps one of the new footmen, the window was pulled up from the bottom.

Even as she stood staring, the man slipped into the room and turning round he pulled the window back down behind him.

It was then when she could just faintly see his face in the moonlight, Alena realised that he was a stranger.

It flashed through her mind that he could well be a burglar.

Because she was frightened, her voice trembled as she blurted out,

"Who are you and what do you want?"

The man started and turned towards her.

"Who are *you*?" he retorted. "And what on earth are you doing here?"

"This is *my* house," replied Alena, "and why have you climbed in through the window? Are you a burglar?"

"*Your* house!" the man exclaimed in astonishment. "But the house is empty – there is no one living here."

"How do you know that?" she demanded.

She thought, although she could really not see, that he was smiling.

"I have been calling here for quite some time," he replied, "and so far I have never met a single soul. So I rather doubt that you are the proprietor."

"But I am," she persisted, "and if you are a stranger you have no right to come into the house."

He did not answer and Alena thought it was more frightening talking in the dark than if she could see him.

She reached out for the matches and lit the candles she had just blown out.

She was conscious as she lit them one after another that the stranger had not moved.

Now she looked over at him with a candle on each side of her face.

She had no idea how lovely she looked.

She was staring directly at the stranger and he was not the least what she might have expected.

She had somehow thought that if he was a burglar, or perhaps a man in search of food, he would be rough and raggedly dressed.

Instead she found she was facing a young man who was exceedingly good-looking and fashionably attired.

His coat was well-cut and his collar and tie were immaculate.

He was holding in his hand something that looked like a block of paper.

For a few moments they both stared at each other and then the newcomer muttered,

"Are you real or have you just stepped out of one of these pictures? I am trying to think which artist would do you the most credit."

Alena gave a little cry.

"Pictures!" she exclaimed. "You have come here to steal our pictures?"

The intruder smiled.

"Not to steal them, just to view them and to wonder how anyone who owned anything so unique and priceless could leave them so recklessly unattended!"

His voice was sharp, as he added almost abruptly,

"You might easily be burgled and then you would lose your treasures that are completely irreplaceable."

Because he spoke so sternly, Alena answered him without thinking,

"My brother and I had no idea that the caretakers had left. We also thought as the house was empty no one would be interested in our possessions."

"Anyone with any sensibility and education would be interested in your pictures. I have come here a dozen times and no one has ever repaired this window by which I let myself in, nor, for that matter, locked the doors."

He turned to look at the picture by Raphael of *St. George and the Dragon* on the other side of the fireplace.

"Have you any idea what that wonderful picture is worth?"

"It is one I have always loved," she responded.

"Then you should take more care of it!"

Then quite unexpectedly he laughed.

"Are we really having this conversation? Perhaps it would be polite if we introduced ourselves. I am Vincent Thurston and I would willingly sacrifice an arm and a leg if I could draw and paint like Raphael."

He walked a little further into the room as he spoke as Alena rose from behind the writing table.

"My name is Alena Dunstead, and you may know that my brother, Sir Robin, owns this house."

"Then why does he not look after it?"

"Because he has been serving in the Army in India, and our father has just died."

"Oh, that explains it. Quite frankly it has worried me that your magnificent art collection might be snatched away from you."

"There were servants here at one time, I believe," Alena explained almost apologetically.

"It would require more than two old caretakers to guard these treasures," he persisted. "If they were mine, I would require a regiment of soldiers to guard them by day and night!"

Alena sighed.

"I think it would be too expensive for anyone. But I promise you they will be safe in the future."

"That means, I suppose, that you will have a lock on the window which incidentally I did not break but found broken, and I shall have to go round to the front door now and beg you on my knees to let me come in."

Alena laughed because it sounded so funny.

"Perhaps if you ask me very nicely I will invite you as a guest."

"Now that is a different idea altogether – suppose we sit down and talk about it."

"I think that firstly you should tell me why you are here and how you have managed to come so often without anyone being finding you," Alena questioned him.

She settled down on the sofa and he sat facing her in one of the armchairs.

"I have been trying for years," he began, "to be an artist. Although I have a little talent, I know when I look at one of your masterpieces how very inconsiderable it is."

"But how have you managed to look at our pictures without being discovered?" enquired Alena.

"I think it must have just over been a year ago that someone was talking about the Dunstead art collection and telling me that half of the pictures were in the house in the country and the other half here in London."

"That is indeed true."

"Because I was curious, I came over to look at this house and found that the front windows were all shuttered meaning the owners were not in residence. And there were only two elderly people going in and out of the basement."

"The caretakers," murmured Alena.

"Of course. When I made enquiries of my friends, they told me that the owner of Dunstead House and the art collection I was interested in was living in the country."

He paused for a moment.

"A few nights later I climbed into the garden at the back of the house, which was not difficult as the Mews was also empty. Then I came through the garden the same way as I did tonight."

He paused again and Alena murmured,

"Do go on, I am interested."

"I saw that the windows at the back of the house were not shuttered and thought I would peep through one of the ground floor windows, which actually looked into this room and hoped there would be a chance of catching sight of one of the many masterpieces."

"And you found that the catch was broken. How extremely careless of us."

"That is exactly what I thought," he agreed. "And being naturally inquisitive I let myself in."

"If the caretakers had seen you, I would suppose they would have sent for the Police."

"I made quite certain they did not see me, although I soon suspected as I came over and over again that they seldom left the kitchen and if they did, they never bothered to go up to the next floor."

"So you went straight to the Picture Gallery?"

"I went everywhere! I could never have believed a house with such wonderful pictures could be so shamefully neglected."

"My father was ill and you must not blame me or my brother. I was in Italy being educated and Robin was in India where he was on the Viceroy's staff."

"You are making me feel I was very stupid not to have put a Van Dyck or a Frans Hals in my pocket!"

"I can give you a firm answer to that," Alena cried. "You are a gentleman, so you would not be silly enough to steal as another man might have done."

"Even gentlemen can cheat if it is made too easy," he remarked, "but very fortunately for you all I wished to do was to sit and copy some of your pictures, which gave me the greatest pleasure I have ever known."

"So that is why you are here tonight – "

"Exactly, and I have now managed to copy quite a number of your beautiful, marvellous and unique treasures. The one I am actually working on at present is the most difficult one yet. It is *The Piazza San Marco* painted by Francesco Guardi."

"I love that picture," enthused Alena, "but I would be far too hesitant to try to copy it."

"I have been rather successful with some of them," Vincent said, "at the same time when I compare them with the original I feel depressed."

"I think it is very brave of you to care so much for your art that you risked being dragged off to prison if you were caught. Were you really coming to work here this evening?"

"Only for a little while. I had been to a party that ended later than was expected. Actually I was on my way home when I thought I would just take a last look at *The Piazza San Marco*."

Alena laughed.

"I suppose if I behaved generously, I should permit you to go upstairs to the Picture Gallery now."

"I am perfectly content to sit here looking at *you*. I don't believe that you are real and I am not dreaming. You must have stepped out of one of your own pictures!"

"That is such a lovely compliment," Alena blushed. "And I am sorry it is not true."

"How is it possible," asked Vincent, "that one man could be fortunate enough to own the most marvellous art collection in the world – but also to own you!"

Alena laughed again.

"I don't think my brother would compare me with his pictures and please don't put the idea into his head. He might be disappointed and he is currently planning to give a ball for me."

"A ball here? You will have to do something about the ballroom."

"I know, but my brother has had the brilliant idea of making it a Moonlight Ball so that no one, except you if you come, will ever realise what we are trying to conceal."

"Am I being invited to your ball?"

"I think it would be very ungenerous of me not to do so, knowing what you could have taken without anyone finding out, but I think in future I will invite you in through the front door!"

"That is exceedingly kind of you and it is an offer I do gladly accept with great pleasure and please may I then continue to copy your pictures? It means more to me than I can put into words."

"I am sure you will be able to do so, but I do think it would be a mistake for my brother to find out that you have been in the house without anyone being aware of it."

She was thinking that it would also be a mistake for him to tell his friends about the terrible condition the house was in –

Or how it seemed strange that Sir Robin was so rich and yet had neglected to preserve his art collection.

There was silence before Alena suggested,

"I think perhaps if you call on us tomorrow and tell my brother how interested you are in his art collection, he would be delighted to give you permission to copy some of the pictures."

"And naturally I will feel very privileged if I am introduced to Sir Robin's beautiful sister!"

He smiled as he was speaking and Alena thought he was definitely the most handsome man she had ever seen.

"Why are you so anxious to become an artist?" she enquired.

"It is a long story. My father wanted me to go into the family Regiment when I left Oxford, but I had no wish to do so. I told him, as I am so interested in art, I wanted to go round the world and view all the great art galleries."

"Is that what you are doing now?"

Vincent smiled.

"I only have a small studio because my father says I must earn some money first. I have sold quite a number of minor pictures that people have commissioned really out of kindness to the family."

"And you painted them?"

"Mostly their children, their stallions, their gardens and their dogs. It is something people like to have to keep, so my father cannot complain that I am not making a living even if it is not a very significant one."

"I cannot believe many people want to buy copies of pictures."

"Frankly I am not really good enough to copy the best ones. I only copy them for myself as I love them and because I am hoping one day I shall become a real artist."

"I am sure you will if you try hard enough, but you have set yourself a most difficult task."

She was thinking of the Francesco Guardi and she had always thought that it was a very beautiful although complicated picture.

"There I agree with you," replied Vincent.

"You are reading my thoughts!" Alena exclaimed.

"It is what a great many people have thought before

you, and now I am determined to start on something very much easier, which I might do well enough to sell."

"Why not a Gainsborough?" Alena asked. "I have always thought that some of his paintings are so lovely and romantic and would beautify dull rooms."

"Very true. I had not thought of that myself, but I will try it. Perhaps his landscape with the mother carrying a baby and the reclining peasant would be a best-seller."

"I am sure it would be," Alena said enthusiastically. "And why not the landscape *The Cattle at the Watering Place*?"

Vincent wrinkled his nose.

"Not cattle – horses, yes. I would love to become another Stubbs. What I would really like to do and to do it for you, is *The Little Girl with the Dog and the Pitcher*. Do you remember that one?"

"Of course I remember it. It is upstairs, but not in the Picture Gallery. It is actually in my bedroom."

"That is why I missed it. I had thought if I went into any of the bedrooms, it would be intruding on my host who did not know I was an uninvited guest. So I kept to the Picture Gallery and reception rooms upstairs."

Alena thought this was nice of him and she smiled,

"When you are ready to do that particular picture, I will have it moved. Then you can sit in front of it as long as you like and no one will disturb you."

"This is really one of the most exciting things that has ever happened to me. I can only thank you from the very bottom of my heart, and hope you will forgive me for frightening you by coming in so surreptitiously."

"I would have been very much more frightened if you had been a burglar and I will have the window mended tomorrow morning."

"Then I shall have to ring the front door bell!"

"And you will be welcomed every time as soon as you have called on my brother."

"But I am not to say that we have already met?"

"No, you must not. I had not been in London for a long time until I came here recently with Robin. He knows I have not seen my father's and mother's friends for years."

"Very well, I will be a complete stranger. But I am sure I can say that my father was a friend of your father."

"Yes, of course, and then there will be no further difficulties."

Alena rose to her feet.

"Don't forget when you do call tomorrow morning, that you have come to ask my brother if you can see his pictures as you are so interested in all you have heard about them and you particularly want to view the Raphael."

She pointed to it with her finger as she spoke.

"Who could not want to see anything so brilliant?" Vincent asked. "I have often imagined myself riding on a white horse and killing the dragon that has prevented me from doing everything I really want to do in life."

"And what is your particular dragon?"

"I suppose it is lack of money – "

It was with difficulty that Alena prevented herself from telling him it was her dragon too.

"It has prevented me from going round the world as I wanted and visiting Venice and all the other places that are so brilliantly depicted here."

"I am sure if you are clever, Mr. Thurston, you will soon make enough money to be able to do so."

"I hope you are prophesying truly for me and that I will not be disappointed."

Vincent had risen with Alena.

Now he bent forward and took her hand in his.

"Thank you, thank you. You are just an angel from Heaven or a Greek Goddess from Olympus come to help me when I most needed it and I can only say that I am most indebted to you."

He kissed her hand as he finished speaking and she actually felt the touch of his lips on her skin.

"I think it would be a mistake, in case anyone sees me, for me to leave by the front door. It would be safer for me to go back the way I came in, unless you have any deep objections."

"No, of course not, and I am sure you are right in thinking we should not take any risks."

"I would never want anything I did to hurt you," he said, "because you are so beautiful, so kind and so perfect in every possible way. And I am going to stay awake all night wondering how I could ever be skilful enough as an artist to depict you on canvas."

Alena smiled at him.

"At least you can try, but not for the moment, as I am far too busy."

"I am prepared to wait. In the meantime thank you again, I am grateful, much more grateful than I can put into words."

He walked over the room and sprang athletically on to the window ledge and then opening the window he let himself out the way he had come.

Once outside he closed the window very carefully.

Then he saluted Alena as a soldier might have done before he turned and walked away.

She had a strong feeling that he would look back, but he did not.

She watched him until he had disappeared behind the trees, knowing that he would find the door leading into the Mews that was supposed to be locked, but it had been left open as there was no one to attend to it.

'Tomorrow,' she thought, 'I must have the window mended.'

At the same time she could not help thinking it had been a most exciting experience.

She had met someone who cared deeply for their pictures – an artist to whom they meant as much as they meant to her.

'I want to talk to him again,' she told herself as she went upstairs to bed. 'I can only hope he does not forget to call as we planned.'

CHAPTER FOUR

There was no sign of Vincent Thurston the next day.

Alena felt unexpectedly depressed.

She had looked forward to seeing him and talking to him about the pictures.

It had been such an amusing incident – the man she thought was a burglar had turned out to be an artist!

She had, of course, said nothing to Robin.

She had merely waited for the doorbell to ring and when it did not, she was disappointed.

The following day Robin left the house early.

He was intent on making arrangements for the ball, especially the electric light he was determined to install.

When he returned he was in very good spirits.

"Everything is arranged," he crowed, "and the man who will work the electric lighting for me says there will be no trouble. Later I am going to have the main rooms in the house wired and we will be completely up-to-date."

"I hope it is not too expensive," Alena remarked.

Her brother ignored her and she therefore knew it *was* very expensive, but he did not want to admit it.

He signed the letters of invitation to the Moonlight Ball, Alena stamped the envelopes and took them all to the Post Office.

'Now we will await the replies,' she mused.

She hoped that some of her mother's friends would come, if no one else.

Robin was certain that everyone they asked would come, especially the Americans.

"I have heard of a few more," he told Alena, "from my friends at White's and I would like you to write to them mentioning how I had obtained their names."

This meant more letters, so Alena again spent the afternoon in the study.

Already the house was beginning to look its old self now that it was clean and polished with Burley providing them with new servants almost every day.

Certainly everything looked very different.

*

It was teatime and Alena and Robin were taking it in the drawing room.

They were doing so because they wanted to discuss what should be done to improve the room.

As Robin had said, it would be most noticeable on the night of the ball.

The maids had already cleaned it, flowers had been placed on some of the tables, but the whole room really needed completely repainting.

That Alena thought would be obvious to the guests when they arrived.

"We will have to receive them here," said Robin. "The decorators want to do only the ground floor, but I will tell them to work on this room as well."

"I don't suppose most people would notice it needs painting and that one or two of the sofas are in a bad state," Alena responded. "Maybe we could find cushions to cover the worst of them."

It was at that moment that Burley opened the door and announced,

"Mr. Vincent Thurston to see you, Sir Robin."

Robin turned round in surprise.

Alena felt an unexpected and unexplained thrill of excitement within her breast.

He had come!

He had come when she had almost given him up.

He was even smarter than he had looked last night when he had climbed in through the window.

She thought Robin would appreciate how dapper he was.

Vincent walked across the room to Robin and said,

"I am afraid you do not know me, Sir Robin, but actually your father was a friend of my father's many years ago when they were at school together. He was telling me yesterday what a magnificent rider your father used to be."

"That was indeed true," replied Robin. "And I am hoping I shall one day own horses as excellent as his."

Vincent smiled.

"I cannot believe you want horses when you have such magnificent pictures. I have come today to ask you a great favour."

"What is it?" Robin asked and then added quickly,

"But first you must meet my sister, Alena."

Vincent walked over to Alena and shook her by the hand.

"I am delighted to make your acquaintance."

Alena smiled and she could see that his eyes were twinkling.

She realised that he was as amused as she was by what they were doing.

"You spoke of my pictures," said Robin. "Are you particularly interested in them?"

"More interested than I can put into words and I am going to ask you a very great favour. I am trying to be an artist. If you would allow me to come and copy some of your famous pictures I would be more than grateful."

Robin smiled.

"But of course you can. If our fathers were friends, how could I possibly refuse? I shall be interested to know which ones you find the most interesting."

"I will certainly tell you after I have seen them all!"

Alena gave a sigh of relief.

She had been scared that if he named the pictures he most liked, Robin might wonder how he came to know so much about them.

"Before you go upstairs to the Picture Gallery, Mr. Thurston, let me offer you a cup of tea," she suggested.

As if he anticipated her offer, Burley appeared with another cup, saucer and plate.

He put them down on the tea table then glanced to see if there was enough food left.

He need not have worried, as the new chef had been determined to prove himself ever since he had arrived.

When Alena went into the drawing room for tea she had thought that there was enough for a dozen people.

Vincent sat down at the tea table.

He accepted the tea Alena poured out for him and started to eat a *pâté* sandwich.

"Do you live in London," Robin was asking him politely.

"I have a small flat here, Sir Robin, but my father owns an estate in Essex with an excellent shoot and some outstanding racehorses."

"That is what I want for myself, but I have so much to do first in my two houses that have fallen into disrepair because my father was ill for so long."

"I am so sorry to hear that. When I tell my father I am certain he will want to know why his old friend died so comparatively young."

"I have frequently wondered myself. My father was well under sixty and might have lived for far longer, but he suffered a major stroke."

"I am afraid it happens to quite a lot of people."

"I cannot remember Papa ever talking about anyone of your name," Alena came in. "But perhaps they had not met for some years before I went abroad."

"My father was a diplomat," Vincent replied, "and therefore spent more time in other countries than his own. He was particularly successful in Italy, and when he retired he was sent to the House of Lords."

"I am sure my father would have been delighted if he had known," Robin commented.

He rose to his feet before he continued,

"If you have finished your tea, suppose I ask Alena to take you to the Picture Gallery. I will join you myself later, but I want to see how the restorers have done today before they leave."

"That is very kind of you, and once again thank you a thousand times for your kindness in allowing me to try ineffectively to copy some of your masterpieces."

"I am sure you are a better artist than you pretend to be and I hope that you will show me your work when it is finished."

"I promise to do so, Sir Robin."

Robin left the drawing room and as the door closed behind him, Alena remarked,

"You did that very cleverly, Mr. Thurston."

"It was important to me that I should be successful. That is why I went to see my father yesterday. I felt sure he would have known your father, because he always knew everyone and never forgot a name."

"I expect it was one of the attributes that made him so successful as a diplomat."

"He was also very good at languages and he loved travelling. I suppose because I have been brought up in so many different countries, most of which have collections of outstanding art, that is why I wanted to become an artist."

"I think we should go to the Picture Gallery, even though you have already seen it many times!"

"I can never see it too often, and it will be part of my future dreams if I go with someone who has obviously stepped out from one of the pictures herself!"

"Now you are flattering me and if you are painting pictures like *The Piazza San Marco*, there is just no room for me."

"There will always be room for you in anything I paint," Vincent responded gallantly.

He walked with Alena along the passage that led to the Picture Gallery.

It was an extensive beautifully constructed Gallery running the whole of one side of the house.

On the floor below was the ballroom and Alena told him again about the Moonlight Ball and added,

"I do hope you will come, Mr. Thurston."

"Do call me Vincent and, of course, I will come. I want to dance with you, even though I expect you find it easier to fly!"

Alena giggled.

"Have I now become a fairy instead of a Goddess?"

"All Goddesses must be able to fly – otherwise how could they have come down from Mount Olympus?"

"I never thought of that."

"Of course they flew, Alena, although as far as we know they did not actually have wings like angels."

"Then I am content to go on being a Goddess, but I am most anxious to see some of your work."

"What you are really wanting to know is if I will do you justice, but I am sure you have been painted a dozen times already."

"No one has ever painted me, Vincent, and it is not surprising, considering I was at school in Florence where most people find the pictures much more exciting than the women!"

Vincent chuckled.

"That is a sad story, and naturally I must paint you a dozen times just as soon as we have decided which style of art would suit you best."

"If you ask me," Alena murmured, "I would like to look like *Diana Resting after the Bath*, because Boucher made her exceedingly pretty."

"I think you are much lovelier – "

There was a distinct note of sincerity in his voice that made Alena feel a little shy.

She had thought when he paid her compliments that he was doing so as to make sure he got his own way – to obtain permission to copy their pictures.

But now he was certainly not joking, but speaking seriously.

'It is just his way of flirting,' she told herself. 'And as I have never had the experience of flirting with a young

69

man before I must be very careful not to let him think I am taking his compliments too seriously.'

She talked to him quickly about the pictures they were passing.

She pointed out to Vincent an interesting Van Dyck and a David that everyone raved about.

However she was only too well aware that he was mostly looking at her.

When they reached the end of the Gallery, he said,

"How could I have imagined and how could I have dreamt that when I used to come here night after night, I would ever find you?"

"You are very lucky that I did not scream for help and have you arrested!"

"I think it doubtful that anyone would have heard you screaming. This house is too big. But you have made it much easier for me now to come here with your brother's consent. I am most grateful to him and even more thrilled because I shall be able to see *you*."

"I must not interrupt you when you are working."

"I hope more than anything else to be working on you, Alena. When will you sit for me?"

She threw up her hands.

"Oh, not at the moment! Not until after the ball! There is so much to do and you can see for yourself the house is in a bad state and I must see to the repairs."

"Perhaps I can help. If you have been away from London for a long time, I can take you to places where you can get things done quickly and which are cheaper than in Mayfair."

Before Alena could reply, he added,

"But naturally that does not matter. I have heard

that your brother is very rich and can buy the best even at outrageous prices."

Alena wondered what she should say next and after a moment she muttered,

"I never think it clever to throw money away."

"No, of course, not. That is why I will take you to the places I trust. Many of my artistic friends come from homes with good backgrounds, but they cannot afford to throw their money away unnecessarily."

"Then I shall be so grateful for your help, Vincent, and I will make a list of what I need immediately."

"I will take you shopping tomorrow, but perhaps I should leave you now or your brother will think that I am presuming on him."

"He is so busy, I doubt if he will wonder what we are doing. But I expect you have work to do or a dinner party waiting for you."

"I have quite a number of invitations as I am on the hostesses' lists as my father's son, but I assure you I have always found those parties are boring."

Then as if he sensed he had said something wrong, he added quickly,

"But I should not say that to you, Alena. You must enjoy your debut and go from party to party and from ball to ball until the Season ends."

"I am looking forward to it, but equally I shall miss the country and being able to ride freely over the fields."

"That is exactly what I do when I am not painting. Perhaps one day we might ride together."

"I know just what you are thinking, Vincent. You want the chance of seeing the rest of Robin's collection in our country house!"

"I admit that it had passed through my mind, but I

would love to see them with you. So when you have the time, I will drive you down behind one of my father's best team of horses."

"That will be lovely," Alena responded lightly.

She mused as she spoke that she was right – what really interested him were the pictures.

The easiest way for him to see them was to ask her to take him to Dunstead Hall.

They walked back to the stairs.

Just as they reached the hall Robin came from the direction of the ballroom.

He had been giving his instructions to the team who were to provide the electrified moon.

"Oh, are you leaving, Thurston?" he asked. "It has been nice meeting you. Do come and copy any pictures you like. As you can see we have a great deal to do before we can invite anyone to visit the house, but the restoration is going ahead even quicker than I expected."

"You are most kind and I am so very grateful, Sir Robin."

He shook hands with Robin and then with Alena.

She was wondering as she did so if he remembered kissing her hand last night.

Now he only squeezed her fingers saying,

"Thank you again, Miss Dunstead. I am very very indebted to you."

Burley opened the front door and Vincent left.

"He is rather a nice young fellow," said Robin. "I don't think he will do any harm copying the picture as long as he does not substitute his painting for one of ours!"

Alena gave a cry.

"What a terrible idea!"

"He would be arrested immediately if the Trustees heard about it."

When Alena considered what they themselves had been doing, it made her shiver.

They had reached the study by now and Robin said,

"Don't worry. I had a quick look this morning at what my Italian artist friend has done. I defy anyone, even the most knowledgeable art collector, to have any idea that the pictures are not exactly as they have been for the last hundred years or so."

Alena did not answer and after a moment Robin went on,

"By the way, I met a young American millionairess today!"

"Do you mean the one you told me about whose name is Vanderhart?"

"Yes – Mary-Lee."

"Where did you meet her?"

"I went over to the American Embassy to check the address of an American I was told about at White's. He has taken a house in Grosvenor Square for the Season, but they could not give me the name or number."

"So you met the fabulous Mary-Lee. What is she like?"

"Very pretty indeed, and because she is interested in pictures I told her about mine and so I have asked her to luncheon tomorrow."

Alena's eyes widened.

"Tomorrow! But surely the house will not be ready by then."

"I told her it was being restored after my father's death. She was most sympathetic, saying the same thing had happened in America when her own father died."

"And it was he who left her all the money?"

"Exactly, Alena, and as she seemed so interested in art – or maybe with me, I was not going to lose the chance when it was offered to me on a plate."

"No, you are so right, and I will ask chef to prepare a very special luncheon for her. Will Miss Vanderhart be coming alone?"

"No, she is bringing her friend who came with her from America as a sort of chaperone."

He gave a laugh before he added,

"If she were an English girl, she would have had some ancient fuddy-duddy, who would have been a blot on every party and altogether a terrible nuisance."

"I suppose the Americans really are different – "

"Very different," he agreed. "Her friend is around about the same age as herself and also very attractive."

"Well, that makes two of them, and we had better invite two gentlemen to make it an interesting party."

"I will ask one of my friends from White's, but I do not want too many of them talking about the place until it looks completely different."

"Then why not ask Mr. Thurston who was here just now?" Alena suggested.

"An excellent idea. Although he is an artist, he is presentable and does not sport long hair and a velvet coat like most of them."

"Yes, I thought he was very smart. I always expect artists to look like artists!"

"I have the idea those are the ones who are not at all important – they just want people to think they are."

"That is indeed possible. I will send a note to Mr. Thurston."

She had already taken his address when they were walking back from the Picture Gallery.

Vincent had said,

"If as you kindly suggested, I am fortunate enough to be invited to your ball, I will give you my address. I do not want to be turned away for not having my invitation with me."

Alena stared at him.

"I suppose I should have put that on the cards, but I did not think we might have gatecrashers."

"I am only teasing, Alena, but with such priceless pictures it might be a worthwhile idea."

"I am sure you are right. We could lock the Picture Gallery, but it might appear rather rude, and there are other pictures in the corridors and *St. George and the Dragon* in the study."

"It would indeed be crazy to open your doors to all and sundry and not guard your treasures effectively."

Alena knew that she must talk to Robin about this concern when he returned.

*

As soon as he arrived she told him all that Vincent had said.

He agreed at once that they should tell the guests to bring their invitations with them and he would also engage special watchmen to guard the Picture Gallery and the rest of the house.

Burley agreed that this was a wise course.

"One place I was at, Sir Robin," he had said, "the burglars got in while her Ladyship was holding a reception, and took away every jewel she possessed except those she was wearing at the time."

"Miss Alena is right and I leave it to you, Burley, to

find watchmen you can trust and keep a sharp eye yourself on what is going on."

Alena added the request to every letter that had not yet been posted.

She pondered that in situations like this the pictures were more of a nuisance than an enjoyment.

'I don't suppose that many guests will even look at them,' she thought, 'yet we have to worry all the time in case one of them is stolen.'

*

The next day she left early to buy herself a pretty dress to wear at the luncheon party.

She had not had time to buy any of the clothes she really required, so she spent two hours in Bond Street and what seemed to her an enormous amount of money.

Yet she recognised that Robin was determined that she should be really outstanding.

She also ordered a gown for the ball.

When she insisted it had to be something unusual, the vendeuse called for the designer and he understood at once exactly what she required.

"If it is a Moonlight Ball, *madame*," he said, "then your gown must shine like moonlight. I think a faint silver tulle glistening with diamante over silver satin will make you look like the moon itself."

"But I do hope not quite so fat!" Alena retorted, but she was confident that the shop which had very outstanding gowns on view would provide what Robin required.

She looked closely in the mirror before she walked downstairs for luncheon.

She felt that her new day gown certainly changed her appearance.

It was the blue of her eyes and the skirt was very full so that it revealed her tiny waist.

She so wished that she had her mother's pearls and perhaps one of her diamond bracelets to wear.

But all the jewellery had been sold – even some of the pieces that had been left to her in her mother's will.

Robin was waiting patiently for the guests in the drawing room.

When Alena joined him, he exclaimed,

"You look smashing! This is the first party we are giving, and although it is a small one, we are going to give a hundred more before the end of the summer."

Alena could only hope that the money would last long enough, but she thought it would be unkind to say so.

Vincent Thurston arrived first.

Then Robin's friend from White's Club who he had known in the Army. He was a good-looking young man and obviously impressed by Alena.

They then turned when Burley announced,

"Misses Mary-Lee Vanderhart and Blaise Milton."

The two girls came into the room.

At the first sight of Mary-Lee, Alena knew that she was spectacular and she was also determined that everyone should acknowledge her as someone different.

She was certainly extremely pretty and it was only her American voice, which was a little loud and sharp, that struck, Alena thought, a discordant note.

The gentlemen gathered around and started paying her compliments.

It was some minutes before Alena had time to take note of her companion.

Blaise Milton was certainly a complete contrast in every way to her friend.

She was on the small side with soft brown hair and brown eyes.

She looked, Alena thought, almost childlike.

Much to her surprise she did not have an American accent at all and her voice was very soft.

Robin had arranged the seating plan for luncheon in advance with an American girl sitting on each side of him.

Alena had Vincent on her right and Robin's friend on her left.

There was no need for anyone to attempt to make the party go off with a bang.

Mary-Lee did it for them.

She laughed, joked and talked incessantly.

Alena felt that one would have to shout to be heard above the noise she made.

The gentlemen, however, found her delightful, but by the end of luncheon Alena thought that she herself had hardly been able to say a word.

"Now we have to see the pictures," said Mary-Lee. "It's been my excuse for coming here and I sure ain't going away until I've had a chance of seeing them all."

"You will find it difficult to do anything but praise them," Vincent piped up. "This is one of the most famous collections in England and every one is a masterpiece in itself."

"We have nothing as good as this at the moment in New York," Mary-Lee persisted, "so maybe it's something I should introduce."

"That is certainly an idea," Robin came in. "But to save you from being disappointed later I must say at once that my pictures are not for sale."

Mary-Lee looked at him.

"Then perhaps you will give me one as a present!"

Everyone laughed.

"That is something I am unable to do, but I am sure that Vincent Thurston here, who is an artist, will paint you a picture that is so good and so beautiful that all New York will go mad about it."

"I will think about it," muttered Mary-Lee. "But I want to see your pictures first."

They set off to the Picture Gallery with Robin and the two American girls leading the way.

The rest followed behind making jokes about who should be painted by Vincent and what it would cost Mary-Lee to open a Gallery in New York to rival Robin's.

Alena brought up the rear of the procession with Vincent walking beside her.

"She is very pretty," she whispered. "I am sure you would be wise to paint her before she changes her mind."

"I am going to paint *you*," he stated firmly.

"You can paint me anytime, so do Mary-Lee first, and perhaps she will pay you a very large fee."

It suddenly struck her that Vincent would want to be paid for any picture he painted of her and that would be unnecessary expenditure.

It was definitely something they should not do with their precious money.

As if he knew what she was thinking, Vincent said,

"I want to paint you only for my own pleasure, and, if you do not accept the result as a gift, I will keep it myself and hang it in my flat."

"I am trying to help you, Vincent, and if you paint Miss Vanderhart, it should give you great prestige as an artist."

"I know exactly what you are saying to me, but I have already told you I want to paint you, and no one else is of any significance."

"That is very flattering, but I think Robin would say money is money, and you should take it when you have the opportunity."

Vincent did not answer her.

He was looking at a Boucher near the door.

It was *Cupid and the Graces* which was one of the pictures Alena especially loved.

"I shall never rest," he murmured quietly so only she could hear, "until I can paint you as well as that picture and looking three times as beautiful."

Because of the way he was speaking, Alena felt a little quiver within herself.

It was with an effort she managed to say jokingly,

"Perhaps by then my hair will be grey and I will be old and ugly."

"You will never grow old, Alena, but I really want to paint you as you are looking now and that is just what I intend to do."

Their eyes met.

For a moment it was difficult to look away.

Robin and Mary-Lee had reached the middle of the Picture Gallery and with the other pair they were laughing and joking, even making fun of some of the pictures and teasing Mary-Lee.

She was answering back when Robin realised that her friend, Blaise Milton, was standing beside him.

"I want to tell you, Sir Robin, that your pictures are the most beautiful collection I have ever seen. They are something I will never, never forget."

Robin smiled at her.

"I am glad you feel like that about them. They all mean a great deal to me, and I am only worried because whilst I have been abroad they have been neglected."

He pointed at one and continued,

"As you can see, most of them need cleaning, and some of them need reframing. I can only remind you that Rome was not built in a day."

Blaise gave a fluttering laugh.

"That is true – and so many old Masters must have taken so much time and good judgement to collect."

"Yes indeed. I would like to show you the ones I have in the country, which in a number of ways are even finer than these."

"I don't believe that they could be, Sir Robin, but I would love to see them."

"Perhaps you and Mary-Lee would drive down with me one day. It is not too far, but if you stay the night I am afraid you may find it rather uncomfortable."

He gave a sigh.

"The house has been closed up since my father died and I have even more repairs to do there than I have here."

"I wouldn't mind how uncomfortable if I could see your pictures," replied Blaise.

"Then it is something we will arrange."

He felt as he spoke that perhaps he was being rather silly – anyone who saw the condition of the country house would be shocked.

At the same time it was important he should 'keep in' with these Americans and make it impossible for them to forget him.

As if it had just struck him, he enquired of Blaise,

"You don't speak like an American, although you say you are one. How is it possible you have no accent?"

"It *is* possible," Blaise smiled, "as my mother was English."

"That explains it – I just thought it strange."

"Many people have said the same. My mother was most insistent that I should speak English as if I was an Englishwoman, even though she just loved living with my father in America and we were all blissfully happy."

"What did your father do?"

"He was very interested in oil, but unfortunately the oil fields he bought were all exhausted almost as soon as they were opened or else were complete duds."

Blaise gave a laugh before she added,

"I am a poor American – and that is something that you will not meet very often in New York. Much less in England where the rich ones come to visit, like Mary-Lee, and attract all the attention."

The way she spoke, smiling with a little twinkle in her eyes, made Robin chuckle.

"Many things in life make each of us different from other people. As there are so many rich Americans, I hope you, being different, receive the attention you deserve."

"I get quite a lot because I am Mary-Lee's friend," Blaise admitted. "And she was kind enough to bring me with her to England which is a wonderful experience for me. It would delight my mother if she was still alive."

It passed through Robin's mind that Mary-Lee was very astute in finding a companion who would not compete with her in any way – someone who would not take any of the attention she so enjoyed away from her.

He could see Mary-Lee holding forth to his friend from White's and he was paying her many compliments and laughing as he did so.

It was quite obvious that he found her entrancing and she knew it.

Robin suddenly felt sympathetic for the quiet little American girl standing beside him.

"I promise you one thing, Blaise, I will take you to the country and show you my pictures there even if Mary-Lee has no wish to leave London."

Her eyes lit up.

"That is so kind of you, Sir Robin, I do not want to be a bother, but I have always loved art and I think your pictures are tremendous. In fact I feel overwhelmed."

"Many people have felt like that, and I remember feeling the same when I was a small boy."

"You are very fortunate to possess them. Don't let Americans or anyone else take them away from you."

"They are not likely to be able to do so as they are all entailed onto my son when I have one, and then onto his son, so that they stay in the family for ever."

"I have heard that happens a lot in England, and I think it is very sensible. It is something I would like to do myself if I ever own anything that might be a delight to the generations that follow me."

"You are very young, Blaise, and there is plenty of time."

He thought as he spoke that it was most unusual for any pretty woman to worry her head about the generations that would come after her.

As if she guessed at his thoughts, Blaise added,

"In America it is just grab, grab and no one worries about what will happen in the future. In England it is very different, because you have such a long history, you think ahead for your children and your grandchildren – "

Her voice was very soft as she finished,

"I think that is very moving and something one day America will want to follow."

"I hope they will, Blaise, and as you know they are buying a lot of pictures from Europe. I am told that most of the rich houses in Fifth Avenue have exquisite pieces of Louis XIV furniture and other antiques that have crossed the Atlantic."

Blaise gave a little giggle and then she said almost in a whisper,

"Mama used to laugh because having bought their antiques without knowing very much about them, the rich Americans just jumble them up and some of the rooms in Fifth Avenue look like an old junk shop!"

Robin roared with laughter and then thought maybe he was being rather rude.

"Your countrymen will learn eventually, Blaise, as we have, but it will take time."

"Of course, but I often wonder if you realise how lucky you all are in England. It is not surprising that other countries admire and envy you."

Without thinking Robin replied,

"And we in England envy your *money*!"

"I know and at the same time Mama always thought it was important that, when we had money, we knew how to handle it. Not only for ourselves but for all those who depend on us."

"Your Mama was obviously very wise. What was her name before she married?"

He thought that it could be a name he might know, but before Blaise could answer Mary-Lee shouted to her,

"Come on, Blaise. We have to go home now and as you know, we are having tea with Lady Carson and she will be in a real fret if we are not on time."

Blaise hurried to her side and Mary-Lee started to walk briskly back down the Picture Gallery.

When she reached Alena, she kissed her goodbye,

"It was real kind of you to have us and I am looking forward to your ball. I bet it will be a big success. No one in New York has thought of giving a Moonlight Ball and I am sure going to throw one when I get home."

She did not wait for Alena to answer.

Still talking expansively she carried on towards the stairs with Robin at her side.

When they reached the hall, Burley already had the door open and Mary-Lee's carriage was waiting outside.

The two American girls jumped in and the footman closed the door.

Robin waved to them as they drove off.

Alena had only just started down the stairs when he came back into the house.

She knew by the expression on Robin's face that he thought the luncheon had been a success.

Then at her side Vincent suggested quietly,

"Now all that palaver and noise has ended, we can go back for another look at the pictures."

Alena hesitated and then as she saw Robin go into the study with his White's friend, she smiled.

"Why not, Vincent? I always learn something new every time I look at them."

"That is what I feel about them and you and I know that I am the luckiest man in the world, Alena, because I have found you."

Alena drew in her breath.

Then she told herself it was just his way of talking.

She must not take him seriously.

They walked back side by side along the passage that led to the Picture Gallery.

Alena found herself wondering if the real reason he was so attentive to her was only because of the pictures.

Did he in fact think she was very rich just as Robin wanted people to believe they were?

'I must be careful – very careful,' she told herself, 'not to become too involved with him.'

At the same time she wanted to be with him while he looked again at the pictures.

CHAPTER FIVE

Alena was quietly arranging the new cushions she had bought for the drawing room.

They were a pretty blue satin and Vincent had taken her round to one of his special shops to buy them and she had found some exquisite Chinese embroidery as well.

She draped it over the back of the sofas and with the cushions the room already looked much brighter.

She much enjoyed her morning shopping with him and when they returned to Park Lane, he asked,

"May I come into the house? I want to look at the Gainsboroughs to decide which pictures I will choose as a suitable background to place you in."

"I have a better idea, Vincent."

He looked at her in surprise.

"I think what you really enjoy best is landscapes. Therefore I suggest you paint me first, if that is what you wish to do, then do your landscape round me later."

Vincent was delighted.

"That is very clever of you and something I shall really relish."

"What I am now suggesting," Alena confessed, "is that I sit in the Picture Gallery for you. Then, as soon as you are finished, I can carry on with all my duties in the house."

"I thought there would be a catch in it. But I am so grateful to have you as my model I am prepared to concede everything else."

They laughed and then they went up to the Picture Gallery to find the place where the lighting was right and where Alena could sit comfortably.

"Later you can pretend it is a fallen tree, a stile or a hump in the ground, but if I can be comfortable I can count up everything I have to do as you are painting."

Vincent went off to collect his paints, a canvas and everything else he needed.

Alena went downstairs to see if Robin had returned.

He had left the house early after breakfast and she had forgotten what he said he was doing.

Burley then announced that luncheon was served.

Alena was just about to say there was no point in waiting for Robin in case he had another engagement.

Suddenly there was a sound of wheels outside and she realised he was back.

"I am here," Robin called out as he saw his sister. "I am sorry I am late but I have something very important to tell you."

"Luncheon is now ready – "

Rather reluctantly Robin turned towards the dining room.

"All right, my news will have to wait."

They enjoyed an excellent luncheon and ate it very quickly.

Alena was in a hurry to hear what Robin wanted to tell her and she also wished to be ready for Vincent when he returned.

She had in fact asked him to luncheon, but he had said he would have a bite in his flat while he was collecting everything he wanted to bring back with him.

"Do you have someone to look after you, Vincent?"

"There is a nice old woman who is the wife of the porter and she cooks anything I require. I am fortunate in having a valet who comes in every morning to press my clothes, polish my shoes and tidy up."

"I have always thought how smart you look," Alena commented. "Now I know the reason."

"If I do look smart, I am quite sure you thought I could not really be an artist because they inevitably wear some sort of fancy dress!"

"That is just what Robin said, but at the same time he said many of them dress like artists because they want to be thought one and not because they are one!"

Vincent laughed.

"That is a typical Sir Robin remark. One day you will have to put them all in a book and publish it!"

Alena held up her hands in horror.

"Don't suggest anything else for me to do as I have only just started in the house and thanks to you the drawing room looks passable, but there are many other rooms."

"We will do them all in good time, Alena, but my portrait of you comes *first*."

Alena did not argue with him.

She was very much looking forward to having her portrait painted –

Or rather, if she was honest with herself, to being with Vincent while he painted her.

This morning when out shopping she had found he was most interesting on a great number of other subjects besides art.

Because he had travelled widely with his father, he told her so much she wanted to know about other countries and he kept her laughing with his quiet but sharp wit.

Now Robin had finished the cheese and drained his glass of the last drop of claret.

"We will have coffee in the study," he instructed Burley as he rose from the table.

Alena followed him as he walked to the door.

As they made their way down the passage towards the study he slipped his arm through hers and exclaimed,

"I have more good news for you, Alena, and I am sure you will think I have been very clever."

"I always think so, Robin."

He smiled as he opened the door of the study and closed it behind them.

"I have had a most exciting morning," he breathed.

He strode across the room to stand in front of the mantelpiece.

"What has happened?" Alena asked quizzically.

"I went over to the American Embassy to tell the Ambassador that you and I would be delighted to dine with him tonight."

"You did not tell me he had invited us."

"I forgot. It was just a casual invitation if we were not doing anything else."

"I would rather like to see the Embassy – "

"You are not just going to see the Embassy, you are going to meet the man you will marry!"

Alena stiffened.

"You are *not* serious, Robin?"

"I am very serious, the Ambassador was telling me all about him and as he did so, I realised he is exactly the man we are looking for."

"What do you mean? Please tell me."

"The Ambassador said the party tonight is being given for a Mr. Finberg – Chuck, as he is usually called. I am not sure about his original nationality, but now he is an American and determined, the Ambassador said, to make himself one of the most influential figures in New York."

Alena was thinking that Robin could not really be serious.

How could he choose a husband for her who neither of them had even seen?"

"What I have learnt, Alena, is that the one ambition Chuck Finberg really has is to make his house, which is on Fifth Avenue, the most distinctive and most outstanding home in the whole of New York."

"That cannot be so difficult if he can afford it."

"Afford it! He is a multi-millionaire not only with oil but every other commodity you can possibly think of!"

He saw his sister look somewhat incredulous.

"The Ambassador admires him greatly and says he will doubtless one day end up as President or in some other important post where everyone will appreciate him."

Robin paused and obviously expected his sister to comment.

After a moment Alena enquired slowly,

"How old is this paragon?"

Robin shrugged his shoulders.

"He may be any age from the way they talked about him, but as he has acquired so much and is so enormously rich, he must, I reckon, be getting on for forty."

Alena gave a cry.

"*Forty*! But of course I cannot marry a man who is as old as that. He is nearly old enough to be my father!"

"He may well be young enough for you, but it's not his *age* that matters, but what he is *worth*."

91

Alena drew in her breath.

"I have no wish to marry a man just for his money."

Robin was still for a moment and then he asked,

"Have you thought of the alternative?"

It was an impossible question to answer.

"Please, please Robin, do not make such plans too quickly. I know that our money will not last for ever and that we both have to be sensible, but to be honest I have no wish to marry an American."

"I can understand what you are feeling, old girl, but to be frank beggars cannot be choosers! You and I have embarked on this wild adventure and you cannot back out on me now."

"I only hope," murmured Alena, "that Mr. Finberg does not want to marry me."

Robin walked across the room and back again.

There was an uncomfortable moment and finally Alena said,

"I do hope, Robin dear, we are upsetting ourselves unnecessarily. After all, if Mr. Finberg is as rich as you say, there will be a thousand women waiting to fall into his arms as soon as he looks at them. When we meet him, if he is really going to be there tonight, I do not think he will give me a second glance."

"I rather think he will, Alena, as the Ambassador has already told him about our art collection. In fact he is far more anxious to meet us than we are to meet him."

"Does he realise he cannot buy the art collection?"

Robin shrugged his shoulders.

"I expect like all millionaires he thinks he only has to put his money down. But we will show the pictures to him and your friend Vincent can then copy one or two for him. I don't suppose the New Yorkers will have any idea whether they are the originals or not."

"I think you are going far too fast and anticipating the impossible. I will do my best tonight to be polite and pleasant to Mr. Finberg, but I am already very positive that I have no intention of marrying him."

Robin was silent for a moment and then he added,

"I don't want to depress you, Alena, but the money we obtained to come to London and open up the house is being spent far quicker than I expected."

Alena made an expansive gesture with her hands.

"I am not surprised, as I know the restoration of the house must be very expensive and the extra items we are buying, like the electrics and the appliances for the kitchen, have been far more than I anticipated."

"That was inevitable and, as you know better than anyone else, there is a great deal more still to be done."

Robin paused thoughtfully.

"If you have to choose, Alena, would you prefer to give up Dunstead Hall in the country for ever or this one?"

"I am not going to answer that question. When we last talked about it, you were going to marry Mary-Lee. In which case there would be no need for us to worry about Mr. Finberg or closing down one of our houses."

Robin walked across to the window so that he had his back to his sister and after a while he replied,

"I have not asked Mary-Lee to marry me because at present she is being courted by a Duke *and* a Marquis. She asked me yesterday which was the more important."

Alena laughed.

"I think, if she is looking as high as that, it is very unlikely that either of those gentlemen would marry her. You have forgotten, Robin, that in this country aristocracy marry their equals. Rich though she is, I don't think that Mary-Lee's ancestry would look so appropriate on a ducal family tree."

"That is true, Alena. So maybe I have a chance, but I would find the American twang first thing in the morning somewhat overpowering!"

"I feel exactly the same – "

Robin turned round.

"Anyway, it's all in the lap of the Gods, and it is no use working ourselves into a huge frenzy over something that has not yet happened – so let's go to the party tonight with open minds."

Alena wanted to assert that her mind was already firmly closed – but she thought it might be too contentious.

"We will certainly take a good look at him, Robin, and make him feel envious about our pictures. With all his millions he is not going to find a collection as good as ours in a thousand years."

"I am sure someone has already told him that, but, as you say, it will be amusing to make him envious and teach him, if nothing else, it is something he cannot have however much he wants it!"

Unexpectedly he walked towards Alena, bent down and kissed her.

"You have been wonderful so far, Alena, so do not let me down now. Meet this Chuck Finberg without being prejudiced in any way before you arrive at the Embassy."

Alena realised her brother was speaking seriously.

"I will do my best," she promised.

"And who can then ask for more?"

Robin left the room without closing the door.

Alena guessed that he had gone to inspect how far

the workmen had progressed and if they were carrying out the instructions he had given them.

She went up to the Picture Gallery to find Vincent as she felt certain he would be back by now.

He was there and she saw he had brought all the paraphernalia of brushes and paints he would need.

He was moving slowly along the Gallery as if each picture he looked at would help him decide how he would paint her.

He turned round when he heard Alena coming.

"Burley told me you were with your brother in the study, Alena, and I did not want to disturb you."

"We have finished our talk, Vincent, and now are you really going to start painting me?"

"I have found a place for you to sit near a window and I think the light there is exactly what I need. At the same time I have no wish to bore you."

Alena smiled at him.

"You could never bore me and I so enjoyed all the subjects we talked about this morning."

"I never met a woman with such a sharp brain and who invariably asks the right questions."

"And what would be the wrong ones, Vincent?"

"I will tell you exactly. Most women only want to talk about themselves. If you mention anything else, they somehow manage to twist the conversation round to them."

Alena was listening and he continued,

"Or they will tell you by a flicker of their eyelashes that you must pay them a direct compliment, which means that the following words will be about love!"

Alena giggled.

"I don't believe for a moment that all women are like that – and certainly my mother was very different."

"Just as you are, Alena."

"So what do you want to talk about now, Vincent? When we left off our conversation this morning we were in Russia or was it North Africa?"

"Now I wish to talk about *you*."

"But you have told me you would find that subject extremely boring."

"I said nothing of the sort, Alena, as I think about you, I dream about you, and I am surely not going to miss a chance of talking about you."

Alena laughed.

"A very pretty speech, but I don't believe a word of it. What I want to tell you is that you must get on with my portrait, as a man has arrived in England whom you may have heard of, called Chuck Finberg."

"I have heard of him – "

"He wants to buy ancestral pictures for his house in New York and Robin has already suggested that if he fails to buy original masterpieces, you could paint a few copies for him. Few Americans would know the difference!"

"Chuck Finberg," Vincent mused slowly, "I recall my father talking about him."

"He is apparently enormously rich and prepared to buy us up if we will grace his house. As far as I can make out it is a kind of Palace where he reigns as King!"

"Are you suggesting," Vincent asked quizzically, "that he might want to own you?"

"I would hope not," Alena answered quickly.

At the same time because of what Robin had said to her, she could not help blushing.

She turned her head rapidly, but she realised that Vincent had seen the colour come into her cheeks.

He did not say anything.

He only arranged the canvas he had brought with him on the easel and placed it in front of the seat he had prepared for her at the window.

It was a low chair and Alena sat down and then as she turned to look at him, he gave a cry,

"That's it! That's exactly how you should look and the curve of your shoulders is just perfect. Don't move, for God's sake, don't move!"

He was starting to work and Alena remained still.

She was glad he had wanted to paint her looking at him rather than looking away.

She liked the way his hair was brushed back from his high forehead and then noticed for the first time how thin and straight his fingers were.

In fact it was a hand that might have been attributed to John Singer Sargent whose brilliant paintings of hands was his trademark.

The time seemed to rush by.

Although Vincent talked very little whilst he was painting, Alena was a little surprised when Burley came to the Picture Gallery to announce,

"Sir Robin is downstairs, Miss Alena, and waiting for you to pour out his tea."

"Is it tea-time already?"

"It's nearly a quarter-to-five, Miss Alena."

"Then we must go down at once."

She would have risen from her chair, but Vincent halted her.

"Don't move for a moment! Just give me time to make quite certain that you sit for me in exactly the same pose tomorrow."

His eyes were running over her, Alena thought, as if he had never seen her before.

Then he smiled.

"Now you are released and I swear that this is the best day's work I have ever achieved in my whole life."

Alena looked at the canvas and he had done more than she expected.

Although he had only produced a little preliminary work on her face, she thought it was already very like her.

"You are not to look," Vincent protested. "You are not to take any interest in it until I have finished. I do hate people trying to help with their suggestions before I have completed what I intend to do."

"I do promise I won't. Come on, Vincent, and have your tea or Robin will think we are neglecting him."

She hurried down the Picture Gallery with Vincent following her.

He had pulled off the smock he wore when painting and put on his jacket.

He caught up with Alena on the stairs.

"I have never had such a happy afternoon and I do not know how to thank you, Alena."

"I enjoyed it too, Vincent."

They were halfway down the stairs when Vincent stopped and Alena looked up at him questioningly.

"Is it the truth?" he murmured. "Do you swear to me it is the truth?"

"I enjoyed every moment," Alena admitted again.

Vincent did not answer, but his eyes met hers.

For some reason she did not understand she felt as if her heart had turned a somersault.

Then there was the sound of Burley or one of the footmen coming into the hall below.

And they continued to walk down the stairs without speaking.

*

That evening when Alena arrived with her brother at the American Embassy, she was surprised to see how big it was.

She had visited quite a number of Embassies either with her father or when she had stayed with school friends during her holidays from school.

This one was certainly larger and more impressive than any of those she had seen and then she remembered a little cynically that, of course, it was provided by American dollars and that there had been no need for economy.

The Ambassador with his attractive wife received them at the doorway of a huge drawing room that appeared to be already filled with people.

"I am most delighted to welcome you, Sir Robin," the Ambassador greeted them both, "and my wife has been longing to meet you and your sister."

They shook hands and then he and Alena moved away to join the crowd in the room.

As they did so a man came towards them and held out his hand to Robin.

"I was told you were coming tonight, Sir Robin Dunstead," he said, "and I have been looking forward to meeting you to hear about your magnificent art collection."

He spoke with a broad American accent.

Before he introduced himself, Alena knew exactly who he was.

He was nothing like as tall as Robin and not at all distinguished in appearance.

At the same time as he spoke, Alena realised there was a strength behind his voice and it made everything he said seem of importance.

There was a powerful vibration that came from him which was unmistakeable.

Just like Mary-Lee, Chuck Finberg did not seem to pause to draw breath.

He talked to Robin about his pictures, his desire to see them and how much he had heard about them.

He made it very clear that if any of them were ever for sale he wanted to be the first to be told – even without seeing what he was buying, he was prepared to bid for the whole collection, whatever the cost.

Because he was so forceful it took Robin some time to reply.

He said that while he would be delighted to show Mr. Finberg his pictures, they were unfortunately not for sale as they were all entailed onto his son and then on for generations to come ad infinitum.

Chuck was astonished.

"Are you really telling me, Sir Robin," he drawled, "that there is no chance of my ever having even one, let alone all of your pictures?"

"Not unless I am really prepared to go to prison for selling them to you – which I am sure I should find very uncomfortable!"

"Where there's a will there's also a way, Sir Robin, which I know to be one of your country's mottos and has always been mine."

"I am afraid that this time there is no hope," Robin replied. "But I hope you will come and see my collection in London. The other half of the pictures I inherited from my father is in my house in the country."

"I want to see them *all*, every one of them!"

Chuck said it so firmly that Alena half expected the chandelier above them to quiver with the force of his voice.

Then he turned his attention to her.

He spoke to her possessively, as if she was part of the collection he would wish to buy.

Alena had to admit he was quite interesting.

He told her very frankly, without being the slightest embarrassed, how he had started from the bottom and how by good luck and good judgement he had reached the top.

"But being halfway up the ladder," he said, "means to me there's a hellava way to go before I get exactly what I want!"

"And what do you want?" Alena managed to ask.

"That's a secret, or rather something I cannot put exactly into words, but I assure you that I intend to make Chuck Finberg a household word and a reason for a great deal of flag-waving before I leave this world."

Alena smiled.

"But you realise you cannot take it all with you."

"I have often thought that the ancient Pharaohs had the right idea when they were buried with their treasures, but I shall be content if I can be certain that when I die they write on my tombstone, '*he done it*'."

Alena could not help laughing.

"I am quite sure," she told him, "you will succeed. And I promise, if it is possible, that I will come and wave a flag over your tomb!"

"Now I really do want to talk about your pictures. If they are so important in England, think how much bigger an attraction they would be in America."

"If you are trying to beg, borrow or steal them, the answer is 'no'."

"That is an answer I seldom get, and when I do I take no notice!"

Alena did not speak and he went on,

"I want to see your pictures and I want to possess them. But I do see, Alena, that I will have to work out a way I can do it."

"I hate to disappoint you, but what you are asking for is impossible, Mr. Finberg."

"In my dictionary there ain't no such word!"

"Then it is something you will have to learn slowly and perhaps uncomfortably, because, just as the moon is out of reach, so are my brother's pictures!"

There was silence for a moment, then Chuck said,

"Already there is talk in America of how it might be possible to reach the moon. I was thinking that perhaps I might be the first man to step onto it! But instead maybe I should concentrate on your pictures and how to get them to my house in Fifth Avenue."

Alena laughed again.

"You can concentrate and you can concentrate, but this time, Mr. Finberg, the odds are hopelessly against you and the gate is closed."

"Shall we take a *bet* on it?"

"You will lose your money."

"I will risk it, Alena, and I will bet you a thousand dollars to one golden guinea that I gain my own way!"

"I will take it!"

*

Driving home very much later that night Alena had to admit that she had enjoyed the party.

They had danced after dinner.

She found that Chuck Finberg, although he might be as old as Robin had suggested, was a very good dancer.

However, she had enjoyed more than anything else dancing with Vincent who, much to her surprise, had also been invited.

The band played a slow dreamy waltz and when it had come to an end, they walked out into the garden.

Lit with fairy lights and Chinese lanterns hanging from every tree it was very romantic.

"Are you enjoying yourself?" Vincent asked her.

"Very much more than I expected. This is my first ball and I was afraid I might be a wallflower. But I have danced every dance."

"They should all have been with me, but you have too many admirers. I have a feeling that after tomorrow I will have to work very hard to keep you all to myself."

"You know that your portrait of me comes before anything else," Alena muttered.

"I wish I thought you meant that," he replied. "But I know, if nothing else, it will be the finest and the most beautiful work I have ever completed."

"Then I am most honoured, Vincent."

When they decided to return home, Robin offered Vincent a lift in his carriage.

Robin appeared to be lost in his own thoughts and when they reached Dunstead House, he told the coachman to take Vincent on to his flat.

Then he walked inside without saying goodnight to him.

Vincent had Alena's hand in his.

"Good night my beautiful inspiration, my Goddess at whose feet I worship," he mumbled softly.

"I will come to you in the Picture Gallery about ten thirty tomorrow morning," suggested Alena. "Unless, you have something else to do."

"I shall be waiting for you," Vincent answered her, "and try not to forget me when you dream of dollars."

"I shall be dream of nothing of the sort," retorted Alena. "It is Robin who will be doing that!"

She smiled at Vincent as she spoke and hurried into the house.

The carriage drove off and Burley closed the door.

Robin had already reached the top of the stairs and he waited until Alena joined him and sighed,

"I enjoyed this evening and loved the dancing."

"What did you think of Chuck, Alena?"

"He is quite unlike anyone that I have ever met, but extremely egotistical and full of his own self-importance. I think that you will have to hold on tight to all our pictures, otherwise he will somehow attempt to magic them out of the house!"

"He is prepared to pay me *anything* I ask for them."

As if she knew what he was thinking, Alena cried,

"*No*, Robin, No! You are not to do that again."

Robin sighed.

"Of course you are right. But equally the mountain of dollars he has offered me dazzles my eyes."

"As long as they do not dazzle your brain, it is not too important. And you know as well as I do the collection belongs to England as well as us and it is just utterly and completely impossible for you to dispose of any more of the pictures in any way."

Robin sighed again.

"I suppose you are right. Goodnight, dearest Alena. You looked very beautiful tonight, as everyone told me."

"I am so glad, Robin, and I do know that I am not as expensive or as valuable as our pictures!"

She closed her door before Robin could reply.

She heard him laughing as he walked along to his own room.

Once she was in bed Alena found it difficult to go to sleep.

She kept thinking of the party and Chuck Finberg.

She recalled how much she had enjoyed her dances.

There had been three with Vincent and many others had asked her to dance, including the Ambassador himself and as there were so many guests, Alena felt honoured by his invitation.

"I feel that you should be dancing with one of your distinguished guests," she muttered as he moved her round the room.

"I am dancing with the one who is undoubtedly the most beautiful," he answered her. "If we took a vote from everyone here, I know you would come out on top!"

"That is the most flattering compliment I have ever been paid and I shall remember it. Thank you very much."

The Ambassador laughed.

"I understand from your brother that this is the first party you have attended in London and I am sure you don't realise you have already made a great number of women know that you have pipped them at the post."

Alena smiled at him.

"One lesson I have learned about Americans is that they pay the most extraordinary compliments."

"I am being very sincere, and I am quite sure that Chuck Finberg and many others here will agree with me."

Alena felt that it was all due to the very attractive

gown she had worn – it was one she had purchased from Bond Street when she had arrived in London.

Robin wanted her to look spectacular and she knew that she was without in any way being in bad taste.

One or two guests had already come to her to say that they knew her mother and father.

Without being conceited she knew she had been a success at the party.

Many of the guests had noticed her and then as she thought how exciting it all was, she remembered just what Robin had said about finding her a husband.

She had glanced across the room at Chuck Finberg and she could hear his voice with its strong nasal accent ringing out louder than anyone else's.

Even as she looked at him, she felt herself shudder.

It was one thing to find him interesting, unusual, and obviously, as Robin would say, 'a go-getter.'

It was another thing altogether to just imagine him touching or kissing her.

It was then quite suddenly that Alena had felt she wanted to go home.

Now snuggled down in her bed she thought she had been rather stupid.

She was quite certain the majority of guests there would stay until the early hours of the morning, but when she said she wanted to go, Robin had been only too glad as he had so much to do the next day.

Vincent had appeared at her side the moment she stopped dancing.

"I think we should go home," Alena said to him.

"I am ready to go at any moment," Vincent replied, "I want to feel fresh and alert for my painting."

Now she thought it rather touching of him to care so much about her picture.

Then she told herself that, like Chuck Finberg, he was obsessed by Robin's art collection.

Unexpectedly she asked herself if that was the real reason why Vincent was so insistent on painting her.

As all the pictures meant so much to him, like Mr. Finberg, he would do anything to be the possessor of them.

But as he could not, the nearest to it was to be able to come to the Picture Gallery every day to paint her.

She did not know why, but she wanted more.

But what that was she could not put into words.

She only knew that however much Robin might put pressure on her, she could not and would not marry Chuck Finberg.

Then she told herself she was being absurd.

Pictures or no pictures she was very certain that Mr. Finberg had no wish at all to marry her – or for that matter anyone else.

He was climbing to the top of the tree and when he reached the summit, he wanted to be standing there alone.

Alena felt that she was quite safe, but at the same time it was something she had to make Robin believe.

When he had suggested that they should both marry very rich people, she had easily acquiesced largely because she had not really thought out what it might entail.

It would of course save them, save their houses and save the pictures.

But it also meant belonging to a man she did not love in any way.

She had always thought of love as something very precious, very perfect and undeniably spiritual.

She could hardly expect it to be like that if she gave herself to a man 'for better or worse,' simply because he was a millionaire.

It was then Alena realised that what she wanted was the love that had always been in her dreams.

The love which comes from one's head as well as from one's soul.

Whether one was rich or poor was immaterial.

What mattered was that one was receiving and at the same time giving something supremely wonderful.

Something so precious, so perfect and so Holy that it could never ever be expressed in anything so mundane as money.

She turned over on her pillows.

'Please God, please,' she prayed, 'bring me love. The love that is more important than anything else in the whole wide world.'

CHAPTER SIX

Alena awoke and realised that she had overslept.

She had taken a long time to drift off into sleep and after she had finally dropped off, she remembered nothing until she opened her eyes.

Bright sunshine was streaming in through the sides of the curtains.

She was aware of a feeling in the air that told her it was far later than she usually woke.

With an effort she turned round to look at the clock beside her bed and started when she saw that it was after ten o'clock.

She would have to hurry herself if she was not to keep Vincent waiting.

She put out her hand to the bell that would summon her maid to the room.

As she did so the door opened.

She turned and saw to her surprise it was Robin.

"I am afraid I have overslept, Robin, did you want me?"

"I just wanted to tell you something important – "

He then walked over the room and pulled back the curtains.

Alena blinked her eyes as the sun poured in making everything dazzling.

She sat up in bed wondering what was so urgent.

It was unlike Robin to come to her at this hour.

He stood for a moment at the window.

Then he came back and sat down on the end of her bed.

"I have just been showing Chuck Finberg round the Picture Gallery – "

"So early, Robin!"

"He is an early starter. He told me that he always rises at seven o'clock every morning. Otherwise he would never get through the day."

"It seems strange that he should have so much to do in England."

"As it so happens, he was going to Birmingham as soon as he left me. He is concerned with some machinery being made there, which I am thankful to say he did not tell me all about."

"Why was he here, Robin?"

"Now you are asking a silly question. Of course he came to see the pictures."

"I might have known. I suppose that he tried to buy them and you told him firmly, as you told him last night, that they were not for sale."

Before Robin could speak Alena gave a little laugh.

"It must come as a shock to him that for once in his life his money is getting him nowhere."

"That is not quite true, Alena, because I have, you may be surprised to hear, made a *pact* with him."

Alena looked at her brother then drew in her breath.

"You are not going to have more pictures copied, Robin? It is far, far too dangerous to do it again."

"No, I am not going down that road again. What I have suggested to Mr. Finberg, because he was so insistent, is that he should rent from me ten of my best pictures for a very large fee."

Alena's eyes opened wide and she asked,

"Can you do that? I should have thought that the Trustees would be concerned about the pictures leaving the country."

"I am very aware of that problem, so I then added a condition that I think would be acceptable to the Trustees, and is also acceptable, I may say, to Chuck Finberg."

"And what might that be?"

She was thinking as she spoke that she was certain Robin was taking risks, and it would cause a great deal of trouble and undoubtedly make many more people realise how desperately poor they really were.

Robin was silent for a moment before he added,

"Chuck Finberg agreed to rent the pictures and to guarantee their return – *he will marry you.*"

He spoke quietly and for a moment Alena thought she could not have heard him correctly.

Then she screamed,

"*Marry me*! You have told Mr. Finberg that to loan the pictures he must marry me!"

"That is what he has agreed," Robin persisted. "I think myself it is an excellent idea and very practical."

"It is nothing of the sort," gasped Alena. "I have to marry him and I have *no* wish to do so!"

She gasped again.

"It is not me he wants, it is only so that he can get his greedy hands on the pictures."

"You can hardly expect him to fall in love with you the moment he saw you," Robin smiled sarcastically, "but he did say he thought you very beautiful and he would be most honoured to have you as his wife."

111

"He only wants me as his wife so that he can show off our pictures to loads of people in New York who will not appreciate them! *I refuse*. Do you hear me, Robin, I absolutely refuse to marry this man."

"Very well then, Alena, if you want to starve, you are going the right way about it. To be frank with you we have very little money left and, as you well know, nothing else to sell."

There was a prolonged silence while she wondered what she should say.

Finally in a hesitant voice he could hardly hear she countered,

"What about you, Robin? I thought you were going to marry Mary-Lee."

"I am taking her driving today and I will propose to her then."

"Do you think she might accept you?"

"I think it most unlikely. I am not important enough Socially and, unlike Chuck Finberg, she is not particularly interested in my pictures."

Again there was another silence till Alena groaned,

"I just cannot marry him. How can I marry a man I have never seen until I met him last night?"

"I think you will find that he will treasure you as he treasures the pictures, and remember they are only loaned to him if he takes you with them."

"I don't want to think about it at all, the whole idea makes me feel *sick*."

"You will feel much sicker, my dear Alena, if we are forced to return to the country and try to survive in the house with no servants and no food. I am not exaggerating when I say we have very little money left."

"I thought you were gambling on a certainty – "

"I thought so myself," he admitted, "but there have been so many items we had to buy and so many wages to pay that the money has just slipped away."

Alena was thinking how much needed to be done to the house in the country before they could even attempt to live in it.

It passed through her mind they would have to let the house fall down and they could move into a cottage if there was one left in any sort of reasonable repair.

Even then they had to eat.

Once again it would be a question of a rabbit, if one could afford to shoot one, or setting a trap every day.

'I cannot bear it,' she screamed inwardly.

Robin had been silent, knowing what was turning over in her mind.

He now rose to his feet.

"Mr. Finberg said if he was back from Birmingham in time for tea he would call then or perhaps a little later. He hoped we would both join him for dinner this evening."

He walked towards the door.

"And that is one good meal I have no intention of missing. In the meantime I will have seen Mary-Lee."

He did not wait for Alena to reply but left the room.

She put both her hands over her eyes.

What could she do.

How could she face such a situation without having to cry out at the horror of it all?

The door opened and her maid came in.

"I were just about to call on you, Miss Alena," she said, "when I sees Sir Robin was with you, so I waited till he left. Mr. Burley asked me to tell you that Mr. Thurston be here and has gone up to the Picture Gallery."

Alena was about to say she must hurry as she was keeping him waiting.

Then she had an idea.

She jumped quickly out of her bed and ran to the French secretaire that stood in a corner of her bedroom and hurriedly wrote a note.

It read,

"*I want to show you the pictures at Dunstead Hall in the country.*

As it is such a lovely day, could you possibly find a carriage of some sort to take us there?

If you can, I will order a picnic luncheon which we can eat on the way.

Alena."

She put the note in an envelope and addressed it to Vincent.

Then she gave it to the maid.

"Take this to Mr. Thurston, and wait for an answer. Tell him that I overslept and am only just dressing."

"I'll do that, miss."

She took the note and left the room.

Alena stood looking out of the window, thinking it would take them some time to reach the Hall and a long time there as Vincent would wish to see all the pictures.

If she managed to linger a little on the way back she would not be here when Chuck Finberg arrived to propose to her.

Even as she thought of it she knew that was not the right word.

Robin had already proposed to Chuck Finberg on her behalf and *he* had accepted.

'How can I do it? How can I do such a thing?' she was asking herself again.

The maid seemed to be away a long time and Alena was already half dressed when she returned.

"Mr. Thurston has gone off to find what you asked him to find, miss, and he said I was to tell you it were quite easy and he'll be back in half-an-hour."

Alena was surprised but she did not say so.

He had been so knowledgeable on art and paintings and she supposed he also knew where he could hire a horse and carriage.

She put on her prettiest new dress with a little coat to wear over it in case she was cold.

Then she arranged one of her new hats on her head.

She hoped Vincent would admire her in it and not think it overly smart.

She felt excited at the idea of going out with him and then she remembered it might be for the last time.

He would not be at all interested in her if she was engaged to Chuck Finberg.

And he would be horrified at ten of their precious pictures going to America even on loan.

Alena was sure that there would be a tremendous row when the Trustees found out what was happening.

She supposed that Robin would say nothing to them until they were well away from England on the Atlantic.

Then she felt that they might be more appeased by the fact that if Robin had money, he would be able to clean and restore the pictures that were left – and to do more than he had done already to repair the house in London and then make a start on the one in the country.

'It is all about *money, money, money*!' she thought. 'I hate to think about it and I hate to be without it!'

The maid handed her a handbag.

Alena had earlier sent her downstairs to tell Burley that she wanted a luncheon picnic basket for two.

She had no idea if there was a picnic basket in the house, but she knew Burley in his usual subtle way would provide her with whatever she required.

It flashed through her mind that if she refused to marry Chuck Finberg, Burley would have to be sacked.

He had done so much for them already and he was obviously enjoying being at Dunstead House.

He would have to go back to White's or find other employment and of course everyone in the house would be affected.

Alena felt as if they were all pleading with her to do what Robin wanted.

It was finally with an effort did she manage to walk quietly down the stairs.

She went into the study to await Vincent's arrival.

She did not have to wait long.

She had only just sat down at the desk and started opening some of the letters, nearly all of them acceptances or refusals for the ball.

Then Burley came in to announce,

"Mr. Thurston is here, Miss Alena. As he doesn't want to leave the horses, will you kindly go out to him?"

Alena jumped up eagerly.

"Yes, of course, I will. Thank you, Burley."

She hurried down the passage, across the hall and out through the front door.

As she saw what was waiting for her outside, her eyes widened.

She had expected Vincent to have hired a carriage that was reasonably comfortable and drawn by two horses.

Outside stood a smart and up-to-date chaise drawn by four horses that were well-matched and well bred.

Vincent was in the driving seat holding the reins.

Alena climbed up beside him, seeing with a sense of relief that there was no groom.

"I've put the picnic basket in the back, miss," said Burley. "I hopes you'll have a happy day in the country."

"I am sure we will, Burley."

As they drove off she turned to Vincent,

"Wherever did you find these magnificent horses? How could you be so clever?"

Vincent smiled.

"Good morning, my beautiful Goddess. How could I offer you anything but the best?"

"How did you manage it?" Alena persisted.

"It was easier than it would have been on any other day. My father had to come up to London yesterday as the Prime Minister asked to see him and so I knew he would not be wanting the horses today and I just helped myself!"

"Then it is so lucky for us and I must congratulate your father, if I ever meet him, on his horseflesh."

"I am enjoying driving them and now you will have to tell me the way. I cannot believe, as your brother said, these pictures are better than the ones in London."

"I am sure you will think so when you see them."

"But what is more important, Alena, is that I shall have you to myself for the whole day with no interruptions. It is something I have dreamt of happening, but could not believe that I would be so fortunate – "

Alena did not answer him.

She was wondering if Vincent would be genuinely upset if she told him why she was running away and from whom.

Would he be that horrified at the idea of her being forced into marriage and that he was losing her?

Or would it merely be because he could no longer paint her or spend so much time in the Picture Gallery?

Almost as if Vincent was aware of her thoughts, he remarked,

"Now this is to be a very happy day. You are not to worry about anything."

"How did you know I was worrying, Vincent?"

"I do know everything about you, dear Alena. I am painting not only the perfection in your face and the beauty in your eyes, but also what you think and feel in your mind and in your heart."

Alena gave a little cry.

"You must not. I must have thoughts and feelings that are my own and private."

"*Not from me*," replied Vincent. "I will explain to you later, but just for the moment let us enjoy the sunshine and the speed these horses are travelling at."

They were already moving out of the town traffic and into the suburbs.

Then there were the first fields and the City was left far behind.

Soon they were on a road with no traffic on it at all, and Vincent gave the horses their heads.

They moved so fast that Alena was obliged to take off her hat and put it down on the floor at her feet.

Now the wind was blowing through her hair she felt suddenly free, as if she had left all her difficulties and all her problems behind in the City.

They drove without stopping until it was getting on for one o'clock.

Then Alena pointed out a wood just ahead.

"I know that wood, Vincent. If you turn to the right when we reach it, there is a place in the centre of it where there is a large pool. The horses can drink there and in the woodman's hut we might find a rustic table on which to set out our luncheon."

Vincent smiled at her.

"That is another reason why I admire you so much. You are very practical and think out every detail, which is highly unusual in a woman."

"It is something I was first taught at school," Alena said, "and something I have practised since I came home."

"I know."

She wondered what Vincent meant, but at that very moment they arrived at the wood and she was occupied showing him the direction he should go.

There was a rough track, but it was negotiable and at the end of it they found, as Alena had predicted, the pool and a woodman's hut.

They made sure that the horses had plenty to drink.

Vincent brought from the carriage the picnic-basket and two other baskets that Burley had provided.

There was a patch of grass not far from the pool, so Alena spread out the tablecloth and put the food on it.

Vincent opened the bottle of champagne.

"We ought to cool it first in the pool," he said, "but I am feeling thirsty."

"So am I, and hungry, even though I had breakfast late."

"I am glad you slept so well, Alena."

"Actually I had difficulty going to sleep."

Vincent gave a laugh.

119

"That is what I have been suffering from ever since I met you."

"I think really you lie awake ruminating about your picture and not me," Alena teased him.

"I have found it difficult to think of anything else but you ever since I first saw you."

"I want to believe you, Vincent, but I am quite sure you say these charming words to every one of your models, which just is what I am at the moment."

"The one model that really matters – "

They enjoyed their luncheon on the grass.

Then Alena tidied up the empty plates and dishes and they just had their champagne glasses left.

"What suddenly decided you to invite me to go to the country today?" Vincent asked. "I have been hoping and praying for this invitation, but frightened you would forget."

"I am running away," Alena announced.

"I can guess who from – "

Alena looked at him sharply.

"Why do you say that?"

"Because I do know what your brother is planning, and I am praying you will be brave enough to refuse him."

"What are you saying? What do you mean?" Alena asked him anxiously.

"I know that Robin wants you to marry this Chuck Finberg for his money."

"How do you know?" she questioned, looking away from him.

"Because your brother is determined that you must marry a very rich man, just as he wants to marry Mary-Lee Vanderhart."

Alena stared at him in astonishment.

"How can you know all this? Who has told you?"

"My father had a friend who knew your father well. He told my father that Sir Edward Dunstead borrowed one hundred pounds from him when they staying in Paris. He told him frankly he would only pay it back if he could find something to sell when he returned home – and that was extremely unlikely."

Alena was listening wide-eyed as Vincent went on,

"It happened a week before your father went down with his illness, and, of course, my father's friend never did receive his money back."

"So you knew all along," Alena said in a very small voice, "that there was nothing to sell that was not entailed and we were penniless."

"I knew," he agreed, "and I was at first astonished when you and your brother appeared in London. Then I realised that no one but me was aware of the state of the house in Park Lane."

"Robin managed to raise just enough money for us to come to London and for me to have a ball."

She was praying that Vincent of all people would not guess how they had obtained that money.

"I suspected it was rather like fairy gold and would soon disappear. Then I saw how clever your brother was in getting to know all the rich Americans, and naturally for that he had to invent a background of being rich himself."

Alena put up her hand.

"You are far too astute and you know too much," she protested. "Robin and I were certain that everything we were doing was a secret."

"I think it is, except from me, and as you well know I would never do anything to hurt you."

There was silence for a moment and then he asked,

"Are you going to do what Robin wants and marry Chuck Finberg's millions?"

"I don't know what to do," sighed Alena and there were tears in her eyes.

"You know what I want, Alena, and I have exerted an almost superhuman patience not to tell you before – that I love you."

Alena looked up at him.

"*You love me,*" she whispered beneath her breath.

"I loved you from the first second I saw you. You must know that I would give my right hand and my hopes of Heaven to marry you."

"Oh, Vincent – "

"But what I have to offer you," he went on almost abruptly, "compared with someone like Finberg – "

Alena did not answer, she just looked at him.

Her eyes seemed to have caught the sunlight.

She knew now that she loved him.

She had been fighting hard against falling in love with him ever since they had met.

"All I have, Alena, is the money my father allows me because he wanted me to earn my own living. It is not as much as I think he would give me if I married, but we could be quite comfortable on it."

Alena made a little murmur but did not interrupt.

"There's a very pretty house on my father's estate. It's not huge like yours, but small and cosy. Two people who love each other could be very happy living in it."

Vincent stopped and moved so that he was closer to Alena.

"What else can I give you, my precious," he asked,

"except all my heart and the promise that I will worship at your feet until I die?"

He put his arm round Alena as he spoke.

She turned and hid her face against his shoulder.

"*What am I to do*, Vincent? Tell me what I am to do?"

Vincent could see that she was crying.

Very gently he turned her face up to his.

"You do know the answer to that question. Love is more important than anything else. The love we have for one another, my darling, wherever we live or whatever we do, will make us feel that we are living in Heaven."

Then his arms tightened and he was kissing her.

Kissing her at first gently, then possessively as if he knew he would never let her go.

*

It was a long time later that Alena sighed,

"Darling, I think that we should go on to the house and as we have driven this far you must see the pictures. Although I don't want to give Mr. Finberg tea, I think we must return home before it is dark."

"You are quite right, my precious, and I want to see the pictures in the daylight."

Alena rose and carried the picnic basket back to the carriage while Vincent turned the horses round.

She thought as they started off again that perhaps by a wonderful stroke of luck Robin would become engaged this afternoon to Mary-Lee.

Then there would be no need to rent the pictures to Chuck Finberg.

She would be free.

*

Robin, when he started off to meet Mary-Lee, was driving the most expensive carriage he could find – it was drawn by four well matched horses.

He was determined to take Mary-Lee to his home in the country and impress her with its size and his wonderful collection of pictures.

Then he would ask her to marry him.

Granted his title was not as significant as that of a Duke or a Marquis, neither of them had such a large house as he – nor pictures that were spoken of with awe by every knowledgeable art expert.

'After all,' Robin told himself, 'a great number of women have indeed found me attractive.'

He had been pursued by women ever since leaving school and he had always enjoyed the flirtatious looks in their eyes.

The amazing words they had said to him to attract his attention and later *affaires-de-coeur*, if they did not last too long.

In India, as the wretched husbands were sweating in the plains, he had visited Simla with the Viceroy and he had found there were always eager hands reaching out to him.

There were lips that were waiting to be kissed.

He had believed without being conceited that any woman he wanted to marry would be only too eager to say the one word 'yes'.

Of course a very rich American girl was well aware of her value and yet he hoped she would find it hard to resist him should he try to make her his.

He had told Mary-Lee last night that he would pick her up at half-past-ten and he begged her not to be late as they had a good long way to go.

He arrived promptly at her address and was shown into the comfortable sitting room that opened off the hall.

He found not Mary-Lee but Blaise waiting for him.

"Good morning, Blaise. I hope Mary-Lee is ready. My horses are outside and we need to make a start."

Blaise crossed the room to take his hand in hers.

She looked up at him with her brown eyes and said in her soft voice,

"I am sorry, Robin, but I am afraid that you will be disappointed.

"Disappointed? Why? What has happened?"

"Mary-Lee has gone off with the Marquis. He is playing polo and he persuaded her to go and watch him."

Robin's lips tightened.

"I am sorry," Blaise repeated, "I knew you would be disappointed. But that is like Mary-Lee. She is always fascinated by the last attraction on offer. It gets us into a lot of trouble one way and another."

Robin did not reply and after a moment she added hesitantly,

"I suppose that you could not take me to see your pictures? They are treasures I long to see before we return to America."

"Of course I will and I have a distinct feeling that you, Blaise, will appreciate them far more than Mary-Lee would have been likely to do."

Blaise gave a little chuckle.

"I am afraid Mary-Lee is not at all artistic, but my mother was, and she taught me about the great artists. But living in America their works are few and far between."

Robin laughed.

"Come along, Blaise, you shall see the great artists at their very best."

Blaise merely smiled at him and then hurried off to put on her hat.

They climbed into the carriage that had a place for the groom at the back. It had an open hood and yet it still prevented the groom from hearing anything that was said by the driver or his companion.

Just as Robin was an outstanding rider, he was also a most proficient driver.

He noticed when they were out of the City and into the countryside that Blaise was glancing at him admiringly.

"I know you ride as well as you drive," Blaise said as the horses quickened their pace.

"All I want are really first-class horses. In India I was fortunately able to ride those specially chosen for the Viceroy. Now I am back in England I need to build up my stable."

He spoke in a lofty fashion and then asked himself cynically whether he was defying the fates again.

"My father used to take me to the races even when I was very small," Blaise was saying, "and I think for a man to win a difficult and close race must be the most exciting adventure."

"I agree with you, Blaise, I suppose that you have ridden a great deal?"

"Yes, I have and I have had good and bad horses. I am just hoping that Mary-Lee will stay long enough for me to watch the races at Royal Ascot, where I am told the best horses in England can be viewed."

"That is true," Robin agreed. "And I would love to take you there."

He thought as he spoke that unless by that time he was married to Mary-Lee it was unlikely he would be able to afford to go to Ascot – let alone run a horse in any of the races.

Unexpectedly Blaise remarked,

"It must be very very difficult for you with two big houses on your hands and not enough money to keep them up."

Robin stared at her in astonishment.

"How do you know that?" he demanded.

Blaise blushed.

"I should never have said it – "

"But you have said it, Blaise, and I would like to know what you mean by it."

"I don't think I ought to tell you."

"I will be very hurt and even angry if you do not," Robin countered brusquely.

"Very well, I overheard a conversation between the American Ambassador and your Home Secretary."

"How did you do so?"

"I was in the Embassy waiting for Mary-Lee who was doing some business there. I was sitting in the corner of a room reading when two gentlemen came in who were not aware I was there. They started to talk about various people who were just names to me."

Robin was listening intently and Blaise continued,

"Then one of them said he had heard that Sir Robin Dunstead had just opened his house in Park Lane and was splashing out in a big way with a ball for his sister."

"Who said that?" Robin asked sharply.

"It was the Home Secretary. Then the Ambassador commented, 'I think if you ask me it is a sprat to catch a mackerel. He has asked me which Americans he should ask to his ball – and needless to say the one he really wants is Mary-Lee'."

"What else did you hear?"

"The Home Secretary then said, 'well, he certainly

needs money. I have learnt that his huge houses are in a disgraceful state since his father died, and I have been told secretly, so, of course, it must not go any further, that the old man sold everything saleable before he passed on'."

Robin was still listening with his heart in his mouth as Blaise carried on,

"The Ambassador replied, 'in that case we can just hope a few American dollars will repair the cracks.' They both laughed and then a servant told them someone they wanted to see had arrived and they went to another room."

"So you knew that in pretending to be a rich man I was really an imposter. I thought I had put on a rather good performance."

"You have, Robin, and of course I shall tell no one what I overheard."

"That is very kind of you. So Mary-Lee is still in ignorance?"

There was silence and then after they had gone a little further, he asked,

"I haven't got a chance, have I?"

"Not if the Marquis asks her to marry him."

She reached out her hand and put it on his knee.

"I am sorry, so sorry if I have hurt you, Robin, but perhaps it is better for you to know the truth."

"I would much rather know the truth. But since my father did not leave us a penny and the pictures are entailed I have somehow to keep my sister and myself alive. The only way we could think of was that we should both marry people with money."

"I think a lot of Englishmen have thought that," she said softly. "At the same time I do often wonder if they are happy."

"You mean they want real love?"

"Of course. Everyone wants real love, the love my father and mother had for each other. Even though her parents were furious that she did not marry an Englishman, she was very very happy."

They drove on for a little while before Robin said,

"I suppose you are right. That is what we all want – to be married to someone we love and who loves us and to have children to make a complete family."

"That is happiness," agreed Blaise, "and I will pray very hard that you will find it."

"Thank you, Blaise," Robin answered her gently.

CHAPTER SEVEN

The horses passed through the gates.

Alena gave a sideways glance at the two lodges that were both empty and dilapidated.

Then they were rolling along the drive with ancient oak trees on each side.

They had only gone a little way when Alena said,

"Where the trees come to an end I want you to stop. I think the best view of the house is from there and I would love you to see it as the Adam brothers left it when it really was magnificent."

Vincent smiled at her.

"I think you love your home, my darling."

"Of course I do. It is unbelievable misery to see it in such a condition and I want you to imagine it as it was when it was the most distinguished house in England."

"Perhaps one day it will be like that again – "

Vincent slowed down the horses and as they passed the last oaks he pulled them to a standstill.

Looking right ahead he understood why Alena had so wanted him to see the house from this angle.

Rising a little higher than they were, it had the sun gleaming on a profusion of windows.

The centre block, which was the oldest part seemed to tower over the two wings the Adam brothers had added.

There were high trees looming behind the house and

although Alena was sure they were full of weeds, there were colourful flower-beds in the front.

There was a hushed silence before he exclaimed,

"It is magnificent. Absolutely magnificent."

"I thought you would think so," Alena said softly.

Then she gave a cry.

"What is it?" Vincent asked.

She was about to respond when to her amazement Robin and Blaise drew up beside them.

As he pulled his horses to a standstill, Robin cried,

"I did not expect to find you two here!"

Alena found her voice.

"Look, Robin! Look!" she called out frantically. "Outside the front door."

Her brother turned.

Now he saw a large covered van standing in front of the flight of marble steps that led up to the front door.

Even as they stared at it two men came out carrying a large picture between them.

"They are stealing the pictures!" Alena gasped.

As she spoke Vincent put his hand down beside his seat.

He knew that his father, because he was nervous of robbers and highwaymen, always carried a pistol with him when he went driving.

For one moment he thought it was not there.

Then he found it had slipped low down, because it had not been required for a long time.

He pulled it out.

Robin saw what he was doing and he too searched beside his seat, but the pocket where the pistol should have been was empty.

Then unexpectedly the groom who had been sitting behind stood up and said,

"You'll find the pistol, if that be what you're a-looking for, sir, under the seat. It were rubbing against me leg and I moved it."

"Go to the horses' heads," Robin ordered him.

As the man sprang out to do so, Robin checked his pistol to see that it was loaded and Vincent did the same.

Then they were both on the ground.

The groom stood between the two carriages holding onto the bridles of the horses nearest to him.

The two men who had come out of the house lifted the picture they were carrying into the van and climbed in after it.

"Come on!" Robin called to Vincent. "They have obviously not seen us."

He and Vincent started running towards the house.

They kept to one side of the drive where there were large rhododendron bushes, thinking that as the men were busy, it was unlikely they would see them approach.

As they hurried off, the two girls looked at each other.

"We will follow them," suggested Alena, "but we must not get in their way."

Moving as much as possible in the shadow of the rhododendrons they started to run after them.

Robin and Vincent reached the covered van, which was a large one, just as the two men began to climb out of it, having obviously stowed the picture securely inside.

One man was standing and the other sliding off the tailboard as Robin and Vincent challenged them.

"What the hell do you think you are doing?" Robin demanded harshly.

The men had obviously not expected anyone to be around.

They were, for a moment, stunned into immobility.

Then one of them piped up hurriedly,

"Us 'as been told to collect some pictures from this 'ouse, but there were no one to answer the door."

"In other words you broke in – "

Before Robin could say anything more the man on the ground suddenly pulled a gun from his belt.

He was, however, too slow in pulling it out.

Robin had raised his pistol rapidly and shot the man through the arm,

He gave a scream as he fell backwards.

The other man, who had been in the van, picked up a heavy stick and attempted to hit Vincent.

So Vincent shot him in the leg.

As he fell forward onto the ground, Vincent sprang into the vehicle.

He went to the picture that was propped up against side of the van and fastened in an upright position with a piece of rope.

It was a large one and as he reached it, he realised it was Raphael's world famous painting of *St. Catherine of Alexandria*.

"You will have to give me a hand over here," he shouted to Robin.

Robin had by now grabbed the pistol from the hand of the man he had shot who was writhing on the ground.

To join Vincent he had to walk round him and this meant standing on the bottom step of the flight leading up to the front door.

He was looking down at the man he had shot whose

arm was bleeding and he was clutching it and groaning as he did so.

Robin was not aware that a third man had come out of the house behind him carrying a smaller picture in one hand and a heavy long-handled hammer in the other.

He realised at once what was happening and raised the hammer in his right hand.

With Robin's back to the man and unaware even of his existence, the heavy hammer would have come down on his head and almost certainly cracked his skull.

It was then from behind the rhododendron bushes Blaise and Alena saw what was happening.

Alena gave a cry of horror.

Blaise bent down and picking up a large stone she threw it with all her strength at the man on the steps.

The stone caught him in his left eye.

He staggered and gave a scream of pain.

Robin turned round abruptly and quickly realising what was happening, he shot the man through his shoulder.

He fell onto the steps dropping the picture as he did so and it fell over the side of the steps and onto the grass.

Alena ran forward to pick it up.

She saw as she did so it was a portrait of *St. Joseph* by Roger van Werden painted in the fourteenth century and her father had always said it was particularly valuable.

Robin now hurried to help Vincent with the picture of *St. Catherine*.

They lifted it out of the van and then propped it up against the side of the steps.

Robin walked round to the front of the van.

He had assumed that the three men were driving it themselves and then he saw that there was a driver doubled up on the floor in front of his seat.

He had his head down and his hands over his ears, obviously terrified of being shot.

Robin caught hold of him by the back of his collar and pulled him up so that he could see his face.

"Are you with these robbers?" he asked fiercely.

"No, sir! No! Them just hires the van and I drives 'em 'ere as they told I to do. I haven't anythin' to do with 'em, sir."

"Then what you can do, my man, is to take them back where they started from. Tell them if they ever try to steal from my house again, I will take them directly to the Police and they will either be sent to prison or transported."

"Be 'em dead?" he asked in a frightened voice.

"No, they are wounded and they may well ask you to take them to a doctor," replied Robin. "I should have as little to do with them as possible."

"I'll make sure of that, sir. I didn't know 'em to be robbers or I'd never have brought 'em 'ere."

"Well, you just take them away and the quicker the better. My friend and I will put them in the back of your van."

Robin put down his gun on the steps.

Then he and Vincent lifted the two men who were groaning from their wounds into the van.

The first man had already crawled into the van as if he was anxious to hide from them.

"I be a-dyin'," the man moaned who had been shot in the shoulder.

"I very much doubt it, though it is exactly what you deserve. Tell whoever sent you here that the next man who comes trying to steal my pictures will die. There will be no doubt about it."

He moved back as he spoke while Vincent firmly locked into place the iron bar that fastened the doors at the back of the van.

Stepping to one side he shouted out to the driver to move off and he turned the van round in the courtyard.

Then he set off down the drive going a little slower as he passed the two carriages.

Alena gave a huge sigh of relief.

Then she turned to Vincent.

"Let us go and see if the rest of the pictures are all right," she suggested.

He smiled at her as they ran up the steps and into the hall.

With the sunshine streaming through the windows it did not seem to Alena to be quite as dilapidated as it had been when she had left.

But at the moment she was too concerned with the pictures to worry about anything else.

She started to hurry up the stairs.

The Adam brothers had built the Picture Gallery on the first floor of the West wing.

As she and Vincent reached the top of the stairs she looked back to see if Robin was following them.

To her surprise she saw that he had his arms round Blaise and was kissing her.

She did not say anything, but ran along the passage towards the West wing.

*

As the van drove away, Robin had stood watching it until it was almost out of sight.

Then he turned to see there was only Blaise beside him.

She was not watching the van but looking at him.

"Thank you, Blaise, thank you for saving my life, I had no idea there was a third man behind me."

"I could see he was going to kill you," she replied in a strangled voice.

"He most surely would have done so if you had not saved me."

As he spoke he saw that tears were running down her cheeks.

Yet he thought he had never seen a woman look so lovely.

Instinctively his arms went round her and he asked,

"How could you be so brilliant as to hit him with a stone before he could hurt me?"

He realised she could not answer him and he kissed her more in gratitude than on any other impulse.

Then as his lips were touching hers, he felt a quiver of rapture running through her body.

It was, quite unexpectedly, what he felt himself.

It was something he had never known before when he had kissed a woman – and he had kissed a great many.

What he was feeling now was totally different to anything he had known in the past.

It was so extraordinary and yet so wonderful that he could not explain it to himself.

He could feel the divine softness and innocence of Blaise's lips.

The kiss he was giving her was different in every way from any kiss he had ever given.

His arms tightened round her and his kisses became more possessive and fervent.

As he kissed Blaise and continued kissing her, he knew he was in love.

How long they stood there neither of them had any idea.

But when Robin raised his head, he said in a voice which did not sound like his own,

"I love you. How can you make me feel like this?"

"He – could have – killed you," Blaise stammered in a whisper.

"But I am alive and so are you, my darling."

Then he was kissing her again.

Kissing her demandingly, passionately until Blaise felt that she melted into his body.

*

Upstairs in the Picture Gallery Vincent was looking about him with an expression of delight.

Alena watched him with a smile.

He was now staring intently at the *Fête Galante* by Nicolas Lancret.

She knew he was as thrilled as she had always been by the attractiveness of this picture.

The exquisite colours of eighteenth century French ladies and gentlemen amusing themselves among the trees was fascinating.

Then she was frightened that the *St. Catherine of Alexandria* had been damaged.

She moved away to the empty place where it had hung and then she could see, as she had half feared, where the man with the hammer had hacked it from the wall.

He had broken the wires that held it, but fortunately he had not damaged the picture itself.

As Vincent joined her, she sighed,

"Thank goodness we have saved it."

"It was such a near thing, Alena. If we had come a quarter-of-an-hour later they might have left."

"I think that they meant to take more than just *St. Catherine* and the other picture. In fact they might have filled their van."

Vincent put his arm around her.

"Forget it, my darling. They have gone and taken nothing. They will be too injured and frightened to come back again."

Alena allowed her head to rest for a second against Vincent's shoulder.

Then she realised he was looking not at the empty space on the wall where the *St. Catherine* had hung.

Vincent was looking instead at a piece of mediaeval furniture which had stood beneath the picture so that it was hung higher and out of line with those beside it.

"What is that?" he asked.

Alena smiled.

"It's a rather sad story, one of my ancestors in 1520 decided to add another Raphael to his collection. I think at the time he had only three, which I will show you."

"So what happened?" asked Vincent.

"He went off to Rome and arrived to learn he was just a few days too late."

"Too late for what?"

"Apparently Raphael, who was only thirty-six and had been ill for a week, had died. My ancestor wanted to buy any pictures of his he could, but unfortunately those in his house had already been sold or taken by his friends."

"I can understand how much that upset him."

"The only memento of the artist that he admired so much was that rather ugly writing desk from the room in which he painted."

Vincent smiled.

"So your then ancestor bought it in compensation for being unable to buy any beautiful Raphaels?"

"I think later he managed to buy one. But on this occasion he returned home, and it was a difficult journey in those days, with only the writing desk."

Vincent walked towards it.

"It is certainly a strange shape," he murmured.

"And not very pretty," Alena added.

Vincent was examining the desk.

Instead of drawers at the front just the top of the flat surface could be opened and as he was so curious, Vincent lifted the small brass catch and opened it.

"What is inside, Alena?"

"Oh, a lot of rubbish. I looked through it all a long time ago and there are mostly letters that are impossible to read. In addition there are a few bills, but nothing of any real importance."

"These letters might be interesting."

"You are very clever if you can read them, Vincent, because the writing is abominable and has little to do with modern Italian."

"That is understandable, but perhaps there are some love letters amongst them."

"You find out if you like, Vincent."

She walked a little way on down the Gallery as she wanted to look again at her favourite picture in the house.

It was one she had regularly come to gaze at ever since she had been a child and she was certainly longing to show it to Vincent.

It was the *Madonna of Foligno* with the Madonna floating in the sky holding the child Jesus in her arms and below her was St. John the Baptist, St. Francis and a small cherub with wings.

It had always seemed to Alena a subject that must have come to the painter in a dream.

She looked at the picture again thinking how often she had prayed to the Madonna.

To her surprise she heard Vincent give a cry.

"What is it?" she asked turning back.

"Come here!" he called out. "Quickly!"

She ran back to him.

She could see he was holding in his hand a pencil drawing that was only half finished.

"What can it be?" she asked him, even though she thought she knew the answer.

"I found this in the writing desk, Alena, and there is not just this one, but a great number of them."

"I don't understand it, Vincent. Why did I not find them?"

"They were right at the bottom. You can see this is a pencil drawing of figures in combat."

It was a preliminary sketch or study, but even so it was obvious that it had been drawn by a master hand.

"Is it worth anything?" Alena managed to ask.

"This and every one of these drawings is worth a fortune," Vincent replied.

"Oh, Vincent, how wonderful!" she cried. "Robin will be thrilled, and so am I."

Vincent put down the drawings on the writing desk to turn and look at her.

His eyes looked into hers and he knew exactly what she was telling him without saying anything.

"Do you mean you will come to me?" he asked her.

"If Robin now has enough money not to starve, I am then *free*."

Vincent made a sound of irrepressible joy.

Then he was kissing her ardently, possessively and passionately until they were both breathless.

When he released her, Alena enthused excitedly,

"We must go and tell Robin."

"Wait a moment," Vincent begged. "We want to be very certain that these will bring him enough money so that he can look after himself and at least live on the estate, if not in this enormous magnificent house."

He kissed Alena again before he turned resolutely to the writing desk.

He began to pull out the drawings that were at the very bottom of the strangely shaped drawer.

There was a *Study for a Cherub* and one for a *Male Nude* and several for a *Madonna and Child*.

Then there was a *Study of Venus and Psyche* and *Christ's Charge to Peter* that Vincent said with awe in his voice was a masterpiece.

"You are absolutely sure these drawings are really valuable?" Alena asked him pensively.

She was still frightened of being too optimistic or of raising their hopes only to have them dashed down later.

What she did know was that none of these drawings were on the list of items entailed.

She was quite certain that no one had been aware they even existed.

Finally Vincent collected what he thought was all of the drawings and placed them on a table at the end of the Picture Gallery.

"I am going to spread them all out. Go and fetch your brother now, Alena."

It was just what Alena had been longing to do.

She ran down the Picture Gallery, along the passage and down the stairs.

There was no sign anywhere of Robin or Blaise.

"Robin! Robin!" Alena called. "Where are you?"

She thought he either did not hear or was not going to answer.

Then he came out of the reception room at the end of the hall.

Alena thought he was looking happier than he had looked for a very long time.

She ran down the stairs to him.

"What is it, Robin?" she asked. "Have you found something?"

Robin smiled.

"I have found myself a wife, Alena, and you must congratulate me as Blaise has promised to marry me!"

Alena gave a cry.

"Oh, Robin, I am so glad! I like her so much and I am sure she will make you very happy."

"We may be very uncomfortable and I shall have to work very hard, but at least we shall be together."

Alena gave another cry.

Then she kissed Robin and exclaimed,

"You are just not going to be uncomfortable at all. Come upstairs quickly. Vincent has something amazingly exciting to show you."

Robin looked surprised.

"What has he to show me?"

"Come and see, Robin, I am not going to tell you because it will spoil it."

As she spoke Blaise came out of the sitting room.

She was looking a little flushed and rather shy, but at the same time very pretty.

She moved to Robin and slipped her hand into his.

"I just heard Robin telling you," she said, "that we have found each other."

Alena kissed Blaise on the cheek.

"It is the most wonderful news I have ever heard and Vincent and I have some news for you. *Please*, please come upstairs quickly."

"I cannot believe there are any more surprises for me today," Robin exclaimed.

Taking Blaise by the hand he walked behind Alena who was running.

When she reached the top of the stairs, she ran even faster down the passage.

She reached Vincent before the other two.

He turned round when he saw her coming and put out his arms.

She threw herself against him.

"It is wonderful, wonderful news. Robin is going to marry Blaise and now we can *all* be happy together."

She was anxiously waiting for her brother who had by now reached the Picture Gallery.

He was walking towards them hand in hand with Blaise.

"What is the excitement, Vincent?" he asked when they were within hearing. "I thought we had had enough for one day."

"That was only the beginning, Robin. We are now

at the climax of the drama. Look at what I have here for you."

He turned to the table that he had covered with the drawings.

Robin stared.

"What are they, Vincent?"

"Drawings and sketches by Raphael which I think I am right in saying have been searched for, for a very long time. They must be worth an enormous amount of money. Enough, I should say, for you to do up this house and live here in state."

Robin drew in his breath.

"I just don't believe it. Where did you find them?"

"Just right here in Raphael's writing desk that your ancestor brought back to England, but no one has bothered to investigate it."

"I never thought of it. I asked Papa once what was in it and he said only a lot of old dusty papers."

"A lot of old papers which are worth thousands and thousands of pounds," exclaimed Vincent. "I think the first thing we have to do is to make quite certain no one steals them before we can take them safely to London."

"You certainly could never have found me a better wedding present. Thank you so much, Vincent, and I hear that you have something else to tell me."

"I only want your permission to marry Alena, and that is more important to me than the whole of the Picture Gallery put together."

He was laughing and Robin exclaimed,

"How can we all be so lucky? I feel sure there is a bottle of champagne left in the cellar."

"Then let us go down and drink it, but for goodness sake let me put these precious drawings in a safe place."

"I propose that we put them back where you found them," Robin then suggested. "They have been there since 1520, so I think it is unlikely they will vanish before I take them up to London tomorrow."

"Tomorrow!" Alena queried. "Are we not going back tonight."

"I was thinking that it would be too late by the time Blaise and Vincent have seen all our pictures. They are of course not all here. Many are in a number of other rooms."

Alena gave a little laugh.

"Well, I daresay Blaise and I could make up some beds for you and cook anything you can find in the garden, but it will not be a great banquet!"

"I will send the groom, when he has put the horses into the stable, down to the village to see what he can buy."

Alena smiled at him.

"You do think of everything, Robin. It is the most exciting thing that has ever happened that we have found these Raphael drawings. Now you may be able to stay here in at least part of the house."

"Would you be content with a part of the house?" he asked, looking towards Blaise.

"I will be content to be anywhere as long as I am with you," Blaise answered affectionately.

There was such love in her eyes and in the softness of her voice.

Instinctively Alena put out her hand to Vincent.

He understood what she was feeling and took it in both of his.

"I think what we could do," he said to Robin, "is to leave you and Blaise to get the bedrooms ready and, before the groom puts the horses to bed, Alena and I will go to the village. On your first day as 'Monarch of all you survey', you don't want to skimp when it comes to food and drink."

"Specially if the champagne is good," added Alena.

"The champagne will be superb," Robin promised. "Go along now, find us what you can and we will have a Royal banquet!"

"I definitely think we must celebrate properly the most exciting day I have ever known," asserted Alena.

She moved closer to Vincent, who sighed,

"Exciting is hardly an adequate word. I feel as if I have suddenly been thrown up into the sky and I will never have to worry about the world beneath me again."

Then he realised that only Alena was listening to him.

He put an arm around her,

"Come along, Alena, and we will find something marvellous for our dinner while Robin puts away his new found millions!"

"I cannot believe it is true," Robin said. "Are these rough drawings really worth so much?"

"I am not exaggerating at all," responded Vincent. "And you will soon find exactly how much they are worth if you sell them in America."

Robin's eyes opened wide.

"That is a brilliant idea. Maybe Chuck Finberg will be interested in buying them."

"I am sure he will be, Robin. If he cannot have the pictures, the drawings are the next best thing. If he can have the lot, he will be the talk of Fifth Avenue, which is what he really wants."

They were all laughing including Blaise, who then said,

"I feel rather shy of saying anything about myself when you have so much to talk about. But I did receive a rather thrilling letter yesterday from Dallas."

The others all turned to look at her with a question in their eyes.

"One of my father's oil wells they said was no good has begun to gush with oil," she explained. "Not only does it look very promising, but there is another one they have great hopes for too."

"I just don't believe all this!" Robin exploded. "It cannot be happening to us all on one day!"

"I think it is fate, or perhaps it is Alena's prayers," came in Vincent, "which have brought us the luck we have all been seeking. I have my Alena, which is all I ask of Heaven. Now you, Robin, have the drawings by Raphael and, according to Blaise, some gushing oil wells too!"

Robin threw up his hands.

"It is not true! I know that I am dreaming and I am terrified I will wake up with a bang."

"When you do, we will give you something to eat and drink," Vincent chuckled.

He took hold of Alena's hand.

"Come on, my darling, after all this excitement we will be hungry and there is no reason to starve to death."

"We are not going to die," she said as they walked away, "as I was afraid I might do if I had to marry Chuck Finberg. We are going to live, and being married to you is going to be very very exciting and very very wonderful."

They were just about to leave the Picture Gallery when Vincent stopped.

"It is what we all seek, the perfection of love. That is exactly what Raphael was trying to draw and why I was attempting to follow him. Now I have *you* it will be easy."

He did not wait for Alena to answer.

He was kissing her passionately as he had kissed her before.

They both could feel the wonder and rapture of love seeping through them.

Alena felt Vincent was carrying her up into the sky and she could touch the stars.

"I love you. Oh, darling marvellous Vincent, how much do I love you," she whispered.

"And I adore and worship you, Alena, we are going to be blissfully happy together, my precious one. When I have painted you a thousand times, the world will know I have married the most beautiful woman in it. She is mine and no one will be allowed to touch her or paint her."

Alena gave a laugh.

Then as he was kissing her again it was impossible to speak.

*

Later that evening after an excellent dinner which Alena and Blaise had cooked, they sat in the dining room.

Some of Robin's magnificent pictures were looking down on them.

He picked up his glass and proposed,

"I think we must drink a toast not only to ourselves, but to the strange and exciting events that have brought us all here and have made us the four happiest people in the world."

Alena slipped her hand into Vincent's and Blaise moved a little closer to Robin.

"After all we have fought for," he went on, "all we have striven for and all we have found, there is something that is even more precious – "

He raised his glass.

"To Love and the God of Love, who has brought us together and will look after us and keep us not only happy but strong enough to make other people happy too."

Everyone murmured and raised their glasses.

"It rests quite simply on one word," Robin finished. "A word we all know. May God continue to bless us now and for all Eternity and beyond with – LOVE."